NOT B[illegible]RE TIME

PREROGATIVE

It was a small and rather sleepy town, called Ditchmarket. Eight hundred years ago it had been important; later, there had been a minor clash between Roundheads and Royalists on what was now a school playing-field. After that, it was as though Ditchmarket had decided its destiny was fulfilled and had been content to go to seed while other towns grew to be cities.

Something of the essence of Ditchmarket was distilled into the oak-panelled, inadequately windowed rooms of the town hall. There was a smell of dust. Doors creaked, objecting to anyone who opened them. The loudest noise that had intruded here for a long, long time was the clashing of the full peal of bells from the tower of St. Swynfrith's Church on the other side of the market square.

And therefore the tense excitement of today was grating on the nerves of Ditchmarket's coroner.

He was a scrawny man of sixty, a doctor, with thin grey hair and wire-rimmed glasses, and he was in a complaining mood. In this town people died natural deaths, so that usually there was no need for an inquest; the last one had been after a fatal road accident, and had been perfectly simple. But this . . . !

He rapped with his gavel and looked over his glasses at the audience in the public seats. There were a lot of them. There were persons present he had never expected to see in this depressing room, with its dark woodwork fading to black, its once-cream walls and ceiling turned to sour yellow. There were old women he knew by sight, because once a day they would hobble out of their narrow front doors to call on a neighbour, and once a week they would struggle across the market square to Sunday service at St. Swynfrith's. Some day, he would know them better. He would be called in to help them die.

There were men he knew, too: solid farmers dressed in their best but seeming not to have scraped off the clinging traces of the rich black local soil; shopkeepers who ought to have been behind their counters on a weekday; retired people who normally were content to stay the right side of their garden gates . . .

And to these people who were Ditchmarket embodied, he spoke severely, conscious that his voice was too reedy to be authoritative.

"Silence!" he ordered. "I must make it clear at once that I will not tolerate interruptions of any kind during this inquest. I am not concerned with anything but the evidence of the witnesses. Save your personal opinions for private conversation, but keep them to yourselves in here."

The audience sighed. Women exchanged knowing looks and firmed their lips together. Men shrugged and leaned back, crossing their arms and jutting their chins. The coroner rustled through the papers before him.

"The first witness is Sergeant Hankinson." he said. "Take the stand, please, Sergeant."

Burly, peasant-faced, rubicund, the sergeant—sweating in his tight dark uniform—recited the oath in a rapid uncaring manner and followed it in the same breath with the particulars required of him. Then he pulled his notebook from his breast pocket, opened it to the correct page, and took a deep breath.

"At four-ten p.m. on Friday last the thirteenth of May . . ."

There was a sound from the public seats, between a sigh and a chuckle. The coroner held up his hand to interrupt the witness, and cast a warning glare at the audience. The sound stopped.

"Proceed, Sergeant," he said. But the sergeant had been put off by the interruption. He had to take another breath and begin afresh.

"At four-ten p.m. on Friday last the thirteenth of May I received a telephone call from Dr Blankenberg at this 'ere research station on the Fogwell road." He paused as though gathering strength for the articulation of unfamiliar words. "The Biological—Synthesis—Establishment, that is." And mopped his face, looking pleased with himself.

"What did Dr. Blankenberg say?" the coroner prompted.

"That one of the scientists up there 'ad been found dead in 'is room."

"What did you do as a result of this call?"

"I noted the details down. Leaving the station in charge of young Jones—Constable Jones, I should say—I proceeded on my bicycle to the research station."

"And what did you find?"

"Well. there was this Dr. Welby lying on the floor of 'is bedroom, all . . . *scorched* and *burned*."

A simultaneous sharp intake of breath from the public seats, which stilled of itself before the coroner could make any comment.

"Was anyone else there when you arrived?"

"About seven or eight people, sir, including Dr. Gordon 'oo'd found Dr. Welby and tried giving artificial respiration."

"Was Dr. Blankenberg there?"

"Yes. 'E said 'e'd come along after sending for me."

"And . . . ?"

"After ascertaining whether anything at the scene of the—uh—the *mishap* 'ad been tampered with, I asked for an ambulance to take the body to the cottage 'ospital. I took measurements before the ambulance came. Also I took statements from those present, including Dr. Gordon, 'oo said . . ."

"Thank you, Sergeant, but I think we shall let Dr. Gordon speak for himself," said the coroner testily. Was that enough from this horrible man? He almost permitted himself to think it was; then he recalled one pertinent question he had to get on the record.

"What was the weather like that afternoon?"

"Sunny," said the sergeant promptly. "A bit windy like, but not a cloud to be seen."

"Thank you," said the coroner. "You may stand down—I'll recall you later if necessary." He looked down at his papers to avoid the sergeant's gaze, hurt and reproachful that his period in the limelight had been curtailed, and said, "Dr. Gordon to the stand, please."

The audience rustled and stirred as they turned to look at this new witness. He was a fresh-faced young man, under thirty; he wore a college blazer and flannels, and looked as though what he regretted most about being at Ditchmarket was missing his Saturday game of rugger or cricket.

"You are Dr. David Gordon, of the Biological Synthesis Establishment on the Fogwell road?"

"That's right."

"What is your post there?"

"I'm a biophysicist. I'm doing research into the physical and chemical structure of micro-organisms."

"Were you well acquainted with the late Dr. Welby?"

Gordon made a seesawing movement with his hand. "Not very. I only came here six months ago, and my work didn't bring me into contact with him much. But we got on all right."

"You live in the same bachelor quarters as Dr. Welby?"

"Yes, my room is next but one to his on the first floor."

"Dr. Welby was senior to you on the staff of the establishment, was he not?"

"Oh yes. He'd been there since its foundation."

"Thank you." The coroner cleared his throat. "Now please tell us in your own words what happened after four o'clock on the afternoon of Friday the—on the afternoon in question," he corrected himself firmly.

Gordon frowned. "Well, I'd finished clearing up in the lab—I had Dr. Blankenberg's permission to start the weekend early. I was through by a few minutes after four. I went straight to the quarters and started to get changed. But I'd only just taken off my jacket when I heard a scream, followed by a terrible crash."

In the public seats, nodding of heads and satisfied expressions.

Gordon cast a disconcerted glance in that direction, let his eyes pass on to the impassive jury of seven men in the oak-barred jury-box, and looked back at the coroner.

He resumed. "I thought at first it came from the room next door—my colleague Jack Millingway's room. But there was no one in there, so I dashed down the passage to Dr. Welby's room and—and there he was."

"There he was what?" said the coroner, and was instantly annoyed with himself.

"Dead," said Gordon, and had to lick his lips. Another unison nod from the audience.

"Describe the room as you found it, please."

"Uh—Dr. Welby had apparently been sitting writing at his table. There were papers on it, and a pen on the floor. The window, which would have been on his right, was half-open. He himself was lying on his back with his feet towards the window, and his chair, knocked over, was beside him. He was . . ." Again Gordon had to lick his lips. "He was very badly burned indeed."

"Where?"

"On his right hand, and all over his chest around the level of his heart. His shirt was scorched and browned. His face was almost unrecognisable, though that wasn't from the burning—it was just sort of contorted."

"How did you know he was dead?"

"I performed the usual tests. Then I . . ."

"One moment. You're a qualified doctor of medicine?"

"I'm an L.R.C.P." Gordon hesitated, then translated for the benefit of the jury before he was asked. "That's Licentiate of the Royal College of Physicians."

"In other words, you were qualified to pronounce him dead. Go on."

"Well, certain features of Dr. Welby's appearance led me to conclude that he had suffered a violent electric shock, so my immediate thought was to administer artificial respiration, though I had no great hopes."

"What technique did you employ—the 'kiss of life'?"

"No, the Holger-Nielsen. I wanted to be able to shout for help while I was doing it, you see. I didn't know if there was anyone else in the building, as we normally work to four-thirty. Luckily, however, Mr. Millingway heard me almost at once and I sent him to call Dr. Blankenberg on the internal phone. That was about—oh—six or seven minutes past four."

"When did Dr. Blankenberg arrive? Straight away?"

"No, at about four-fifteen. He explained that he had telephoned the police and asked for someone to come over. I had continued the artificial respiration, but Dr. Blankenberg examined Dr. Welby's body and advised me there was no point in trying further. He was past the limit of any conceivable medical assistance."

A murmur from the public seats.

Now the question the coroner was most reluctant to put, but which would have to be asked sooner or later. He sat up very straight.

"Dr. Gordon, had you ever seen anyone in a condition similar to Dr. Welby's, which might have led you to an opinion regarding the cause of death?"

"Yes." Gordon looked at the floor helplessly. "The resemblance hit me the moment I entered the room. I once saw somebody struck by lightning. Of course, out of a clear sky such as we had that day, it's ridiculous. Nonetheless," he finished firmly, "lightning."

"Thank you. You may stand down."

After that came the surgeon who had performed the post-mortem examination. He offered little but a jargon-ridden description of the corpse's state when he saw it, and a cautious agreement that death was due to violent electrocution. The audience looked bored, as though this was to them a waste of time.

"Dr. Blankenberg," said the coroner, and instantly the

listeners stiffened. This, he realised, was the witness they had been waiting for—and in moments he saw why.

Short, podgy, going bald, Dr. Blankenberg was swarthy of skin, black of hair, and the nose on which his spectacles sat was distinctly hooked. He came forward under the hostile rustic English glare of the townspeople and took the stand.

"Uh—are you Jewish, Dr. Blankenberg?" the coroner suggested, wondering whether there was any book in the building suitable for administering a Jewish oath. The audience seemed to gather its concentration, menacingly.

"By race, but not by persuasion," said Dr. Blankenberg. "I am an agnostic and prefer to make an affirmation rather than take an oath."

This time the response from the public seats was a gasp. A Jew was bad enough; a Jew who had renounced his faith was one step beyond the limit. Someone said, "Shame!"—but not loudly enough to compel the coroner to take notice.

"Very well," sighed the coroner. And, when the affirmation was taken, went on: "You are Dr. Joseph Blankenberg, director of the Biological Synthesis Establishment here?"

"I am."

"Please tell us how you heard of the death of Dr. Welby."

Blankenberg took hold of the bar across the front of the witness stand and spoke in a level voice. "It was about six minutes past four when my internal telephone rang. I was in my office, completing my paper work before the weekend. The caller was Mr. Millingway. He said that Dr. Welby had been found dead in his room and Dr. Gordon was giving artificial respiration. I spoke with him long enough to ascertain that it was no mere case of—let's say—heart failure, and felt it advisable to ring the police. I did so, speaking to the person I now know as Sergeant Hankinson. Then I went to see for myself, and on the basis of my examination of Dr. Welby advised Dr. Gordon to abandon his attempts to revive him.

"By the time the sergeant arrived, it was past the time of cease-work, and about half a dozen people had gathered in the bachelor quarters. We work generally from eight-thirty a.m. to four-thirty p.m., except on projects which involve shift work."

"And what was your reaction to the sight of Dr. Welby?"

"He looked to me as though he'd been struck by lightning. Unlike Dr. Gordon, I've never actually seen anyone struck by lightning, but I did once see a man who had been killed by touching a thirty-thousand-volt power line, and he looked much as Dr. Welby did."

"When you saw him, was he lying where Dr. Gordon found him?"

"Apart from the movement involved in artificial respiration, of course, I understand that he was. He was on his back with his feet almost touching the base of the radiator under the window. A chair was overset alongside him, with his jacket on the back. He had been working at his table in shirt-sleeves, because although the day was windy it was rather warm and had been sunny since before lunch."

"Would you say that this type of weather rules out the possibility of Dr. Welby's death actually being due to lightning?"

"Offhand, certainly I would. Though I'm no meteorologist."

"What more *rational* explanation occurred to you?" The coroner weighted the words and glanced over covertly to see if they had any impact on the jury, hoping against hope that they had not —as he suspected—decided on their verdict long before entering the court.

"Well, electrocution. From faulty wiring, perhaps. I did make a quick survey of the switches and other fitments, but they were all apparently in sound order, and in any case no wiring was within arm's reach of where Dr. Welby would have been standing, close to the window." Dr. Blankenberg's dark eyes flicked briefly towards the audience and back to the coroner. "However, I later arranged for a thorough inspection by an expert from London, and I was informed . . ."

"Thank you!" the coroner cut in, raising his hand. "The gentleman in question is present and will be giving us his findings in due course. Ah . . . Oh yes. I gather that Dr. Welby was thoroughly familiar with his room, in that he had occupied it for a considerable time."

"Six years—since the foundation of the establishment. He moved in as a temporary measure, and being a single man and rather simple in his tastes, was satisfied to remain there rather than take lodgings locally, which his salary and seniority would have led one to expect. As a matter of fact, he'd been with the establishment longer than I have myself—his project was the first to be launched when the station was set up."

There was a sudden shout from the public seats. "Devil's work! That's what he was doing—devil's work!"

"That it was!" A deep undercurrent of grumbling began; the coroner had to hammer for silence.

"If there's one more interruption like that, I'll clear you all out!" he snapped. "I'm sorry, Dr. Blankenberg. As you probably know, however, there's been a good deal of stupid talk about Dr. Welby's research—could you make it clear for the jury what he was doing?"

"He was engaged in an attempt to synthesise a replicating molecule from elementary constituents," said Blankenberg frigidly. The coroner blinked.

"Perhaps you could clarify that?" he invited.

Blankenberg looked absently towards a window which framed the tower of St. Swynfrith's. "Essentially it amounts to this. We believe that many thousands of years ago this world had a different atmosphere from the one it has now. It was hot and steamy with unfamiliar gases in it such as ammonia and methane—marsh-gas. We believe that over thousands of centuries chance brought together the elements which compose our own bodies, such as hydrogen, oxygen, carbon and nitrogen, into a molecule—a collection of atoms—which had the power of reproducing itself. Molecules like this are called viruses. The common cold is caused by one. You can't really say they are alive, because you can break them down in a laboratory and put them together again in a different arrangement, and they go on reproducing themselves in a new form. But they do have the power, as plants and animals have, of taking simple substances from their surroundings and turning these substances into copies of themselves. We say they can *replicate* themselves. We won't go so far as to say they are actually reproducing like living things.

"What Dr. Welby was doing was an extension of an experiment carried out some years ago in America by a scientist named Miller. Miller filled a closed tube with the same gases we believed formed the primal atmosphere of Earth, connected the tube to a retort of boiling water, put a spark discharge across it to imitate lightning, because lightning played an important part in mixing the elements when life began on our planet . . ."

The audience was shaking its head sorrowfully. Out of its superior wisdom it was pitying this man who did not know that the world was created on a Sunday in October of 4004 B.C., at a little after four in the afternoon.

"After only a few days Miller found that quite complicated substances had arisen in his glass tube: proteins, the bricks out of which all living creatures are built. So Dr. Welby pointed out that if proteins could be generated in a few days in a small system, there was a good chance of generating a replicating molecule in a large system, given several years in which to operate.

"And this was what he set out to do. He contrived a closed system free from any possible outside contamination, in which he circulated a mixture of the primal gases. He had means of detecting any changes in the contents by spectroanalysis and remote chromatography, and once in a while—usually on the first Monday of alternate months—he drew off a sample for direct analysis, afterwards reducing it to its elements again and returning it to the system to maintain a constant balance of the constituents."

"And . . ." The coroner had to swallow. "And had he had any success?"

"He had had some success prior to his death, yes," said Dr. Blankenberg. "He had identified some very complex high-order proteins, many of them close to viruses."

The coroner leaned back. "You said 'had had some success prior to his death'," he repeated, and glanced nervously at the public seats. The jury were still impassive. "Are you implying that now he is dead the work will be discontinued?"

"Of course not. This is a tremendously exciting project, and it would certainly have been Dr. Welby's wish that we continue it." Blankenberg spoke in a firm voice, but his hands tightened on the bar of the witness stand.

Mentally rehearsing a stern directive to the jury about superstition and double-talk, the coroner nodded. "Thank you—you may stand down."

"Oh no you don't!" bellowed a hoarse voice. The coroner, heart sinking, raised his head to find Fred Warble on his feet—a bellicose man who farmed sixty acres a mile from Ditchmarket, and had had his eye on another ten before the land was taken under a compulsory purchase order to build the research establishment. The coroner had been fairly sure that if trouble arose some of it would come from Warble.

He pounded his gavel, but Warble shook a meaty fist in the air towards him. "No you don't!" he repeated. "Make him tell what they got out of their witches' stew on Monday! Make him tell what shame he's brought on Ditchmarket with his black arts!"

The old women in the front row were giving approving nods. The jury were swallowing nervously and having to tug at their collars as though suffocating.

"Very well," said the coroner after a tense pause. "As a concession I'll ask the question—if only to make a lot of idiotic rumours lie down! I'm surprised at you, Mr. Warble.

You're a level-headed man, and here you're talking about black arts like some—some benighted gypsy!"

Warble seemed to grow a little smaller suddenly. "All right," he said in a grudging tone, and sat down. "But you ask him, mind!" he added with a resurgence of aggression, before folding his arms and sitting quiet.

During the exchange, Blankenberg had remained as he had been when Warble interrupted: with one hand on the rail of the witness stand, poised to step to the floor. Now he shrugged and faced the coroner again.

"Dr. Blankenberg," said the coroner solemnly, "have you examined Dr. Welby's experiment since his death?"

"I have. On Monday morning of this week, to be exact."

'And what did you find?"

Blankenberg hesitated. He glanced towards Warble and then at the jury, and pulled himself up to his full height. "I found," he said in a clear voice, "that a complex replicating molecule had spontaneously occurred in the mixture, as Dr. Welby had hoped and predicted."

Warble's face was perfectly blank, and so were other faces in the audience. Obviously, references to replicating molecules were over their heads. But in that case, Warble wouldn't be satisfied with the answer. The coroner felt driven onwards, carried along despite himself. He said firmly, "How—complex?"

"Comparable with *vaccinia,* the—uh—the infective agent responsible for smallpox." Blankenberg was sweating freely now; his forehead gleamed, but he did not wipe it.

"And this is a fairly advanced organism? Is it in fact indisputably a living creature?"

"Yes," said Blankenberg, and the word froze the air of the room. Suddenly there was not a sound. Not a single sound, not even the noise of breathing.

There were more questions. The coroner pushed the first of the last into the terrible silence. "Have you studied the reproduction of this organism?"

"Yes."

Again pushed into the heavy silence: "Have you calculated how long it had been reproducing in the system before you found it?"

"Yes."

"Then when did it—did it . . . ?" The coroner found the last words too hard to utter. Blankenberg saved him the trouble.

"It must have begun to reproduce itself—that is, it must have come to life—on Friday afternoon of last week." And he finished, his voice suddenly dropping to a whisper, "In fact, at about the time Dr. Welby died."

The faces of the audience were still, like so many stones. They were set in expressions that could be read. Without movement, they informed the world—and each other, especially each other—that they had known. Yes, they had known. At the moment when his blasphemies and impieties found fruition, the bolt from heaven had struck down the man who aspired to usurp the prerogative of Another and create life.

One by one they rose and began to leave the room. They would not stay to hear the evidence of the expert from London who had inspected the scene of the accident, traced the swinging electric cable which the wind had carried against the steel frame of Dr. Welby's window and gradually frayed through, so that when he tired of the breeze disturbing his papers and rose to push the window shut the first shock made him fall against the metal radiator and ground the entire current through his unprotected chest.

They had reached their verdict already. And so, the coroner realised sickly, had his jury. Not a hundred years of expert testimony would alter their intention of setting down on record as the cause of death the phrase in which the foreman's lips were even now moving, as though rehearsing the words and savouring their ring.

"Act of God," the coroner whispered to himself. "Act of God."

FAIR WARNING

I HAD this from someone I met in a London pub, so it's only fair to stress that (a) it's at best secondhand and (b) as the phrase goes, "Names have been changed to protect the innocent."

There was this young man sitting at the bar. I came up and ordered a drink. He saw the pin on my lapel, which I always wear—the sign of the Society for the Prevention of Nuclear War. Pointing at it, he said, "You're scared."

headphones to the tock-tock-brrr of a geiger counter. The case itself was slung in a cradle of tension springs like those used to ship unique archæological relics, and when the boat nosed softly against the shore the men who had to lift it treated it with far more care than an equivalent quantity of eggs.

Among the men who came to greet it on arrival, showing the courtesy normally only expended on visiting royalty, were the two most important men on the island. They had been the most important even when all the hundred-plus previous inhabitants had been here, although there were several of the hundred-plus to whom it was not politic to mention the fact.

One of them was balding and elderly, with a slight stoop and horn-rimmed glasses. He had discs of green glass clipped over the lenses against the sunlight. The other was older, but looked younger because he was tall and thin and stood very erect. As they waited for the crate's handlers to transfer it from the cradle in the boat to another similar cradle specially rigged on the flat back of a half-tracked pickup, the one with glasses pulled a handkerchief from his pocket and furiously wiped first the glasses and then his face.

"God!" he said. "The heat!"

His companion glanced at him and smiled without humour. "Don't let it get you down, Vliesser. It's going to be a hell of a lot hotter in a few hours' time."

Vliesser snorted. "We shall be well out of it by then. I swear, even if it means putting off the firing for half an hour I intend to get a shower before zero hour."

"Stand out on deck. The blast will pick up plenty of water."

"Damn you, Rogan—do you have to be so cynical?"

"If I wasn't cynical," the tall man said, "I'd be shaking like a leaf. Was it this way at Bikini in '54?"

"I don't know. I wasn't there. In any case, this is a new advance. Qualitatively new. What's the good of drawing empty comparisons?" Vliesser mopped his forehead again.

"They used to tell a story to newcomers in the western states, about the bird that flew backwards because he liked to see where he'd gone." Rogan chuckled. "That's me. I'm temperamentally unsuited for major forward steps."

The naval lieutenant who had been supervising the stowage of the packing case turned away from the pickup and saluted.

"The crate's ready to go to the cabin now, Dr. Rogan," he said. "You've been briefed on arrangements for the evacuation?"

Civilians in a target area, thought Rogan wryly. Aloud he answered, "Yes, we've been told. Directly we've armed the bomb we drive back to the beach; you'll be waiting at the boat, and we're to abandon the truck and come aboard."

"That's right," nodded the young officer. "Well, I'll get my men aboard now—I've been warned not to let them stay on shore while you're in the cabin." He hesitated. "Is that all?"

Rogan confirmed, and he saluted and went to round up his men.

Vliesser checked the spring cradle carrying the crate, gave a satisfied nod and addressed Rogan. "You know how to drive this—mechanical yak, I suppose? I didn't think to ask."

"Yes, I took a lesson on it a couple of days ago. Jump in." Rogan climbed over the low door into the driving seat; more awkwardly, Vliesser settled his podgy bulk in the passenger's place.

"Not less than a hundred and twenty people have seen the thing being built," he grunted. "You'd think one of them could be allowed to stay and give us a hand."

"Security," Rogan said. "I'm sure they'd be happier if even we didn't know how the thing is supposed to work. Matter of fact," he added reflectively, "I sometimes feel the same. But never mind. Hold on—here we go."

He started the engine, engaged a low gear, and began to ease the half-track up the gentle slope towards the black cabin.

Vliesser remained silent, mopping his forehead, for a full minute before speaking again. Then, not looking at his companion, he said, "Do you think it'll function?"

"Ask me this evening."

"Rogan, be serious. The occasion demands it. Think! The first man-made phœnix reaction—the first artificial carbon-nitrogen cycle—is probably going to be induced here, today!"

Guiding the vehicle carefully around some felled palms, Rogan nodded. "I hope it does work. I want to get back to something a bit more rewarding."

Vliesser glanced at him. "So you hope it will work? Do you not mean you hope it won't?"

"Not at all. I'm tired of being chased by the military towards bigger and better explosions. Now we've reached the level at which they're bound to lose interest. I mean, this really would be the weapon too terrible to use, wouldn't it?" He waved at the cabin ahead. "Let this thing off over open water, and you'll have a self-sustaining hydrogen reaction. It'd wipe the planet clean in about a twenty-fifth of a second."

"I made it decimal oh-five second," Vliesser said after a pause. "It's a function of the available deuterium."

"Don't let's argue," Rogan said with a wry smile, braking the half-track and swinging its nose around. After a couple of failures he backed it into a convenient position to unload.

Grumbling continually under his breath, Vliesser got down and helped his companion to manhandle the crate out of its springs. Carrying it between them, they entered the cabin. The black painted walls had absorbed the sun, and the heat struck at them like a hammer.

"If this were T.N.T.," Rogan said emotionlessly as he lowered his end of the crate, "I'd be running in case the heat in here set it off. Open it up, will you?"

Vliesser bent to the combination lock on the crate. He undid it, lifted off the lid. Inside there was insulation—a double layer of lead foil; flat cans of heavy water forming a false case inside the main one; more lead, in slabs rather than foil; rubber blocks to act as shock absorbers, and finally the trigger, a slender metal cylinder the length of a man's arm.

Rogan set it gently on the sliding cradle which was to take it into the very heart of the bomb mechanism. He gave it a pat, then produced a note pad from the pocket of his shirt and began to read out a list of figures. As he read, Vliesser moved about him, checking dials and operating levers marked with the wasp sign—black and yellow stripes signifying DANGER.

Everything was normal. Rogan sighed with relief and pocketed the note-pad again. He picked up two leads with crocodile clips on the ends and brought them to twin terminals peeking out of the end of the trigger. Vlieser's breathing was the loudest sound in the world.

The wires were clipped in place. Rogan muttered something to himself and pushed the lever beside the sliding cradle. Silently, the trigger ran down its oiled causeway into the appointed place.

"Now all we have to do is turn on the radio controls," said Vliesser. "Then we can go."

"Light the blue touchpaper and retire to a safe distance," Rogan quoted.

"What?" Vliesser glanced up sharply.

"Nothing. I was just thinking"—Rogan's eyes roved the mechanism surrounding them—"that you were right to say this was a great occasion. Shall we mark it appropriately?" He felt in the hip pocket of his khaki shorts and took out a flask. "Let's toast it, in the hope that it won't do the same to us."

"I can't say I share your sense of humour," Vliesser commented. "But I will cheerfully share your liquor."

"Here, then." Carefully, as he had armed the bomb, Rogan measured out half the contents of the flask into the lid for Vlieser, then raised the flask mockingly to his lips.

And his arm stopped. Everything stopped. He could not move a single muscle except his eyes and those involved in breathing. He tried to cry out, but failed, and from the look of terror which showed on Vliesser's face he knew that the same paralysis had overtaken them both.

A second or two later, out of the side of his eyes, he saw a distinct shimmer in the air between him and the wall. It resembled a heat-effect, but was too sharply defined.

As stiff as though turned to stone, they stayed where they were.

Out of the shimmer in the air, a form was—was materialising. A form as tall as a man, but not quite shaped like a man, although it had the same number of limbs, the same proportion of head to trunk, and moved with a man-like gait.

Straining to see what it was, Rogan felt his eye-muscles stabbed by pain, and he had to look to the front again, where all he could see was Vliesser, a statue depicting raw fear.

About ten minutes went by. During it they barely glimpsed the stranger, but they could guess what he was doing—he was going around the cabin checking all the mechanism which was so shortly due for a fast and fiery end. They heard clinking noises, and shuffling footsteps; once or twice they had a view of the stranger's back as he passed across their field of vision. But at no time did they see him clearly.

They heard him very well, of course. And that was the trouble.

When the tour of inspection was complete, the stranger paused in front of the shimmer in the air and—so it seemed to Rogan—glanced back. A voice tinged with sarcasm said, in perfect English with a strong American accent: "Congratulations, gentlemen! This time you'll manage it!"

Their invisible bonds broke. Flask and lid crashed to the floor as they whirled.

But there was no one there.

The island baked on. Aboard a ship far out to sea, men looked impatiently at their watches. The young lieutenant in charge of the boat which was supposed to be taking Rogan and Vliesser away discovered that they were five full minutes overdue. He contemplated the relative risk of taking a party up to investigate and being court-martialled for disobeying orders, or doing nothing and being court-martialled for not going to the rescue. He decided to give the scientists another five minutes.

He hoped to hell there hadn't been a mix-up in his orders. The island was only baking now; shortly it would be burned to a crisp. Possibly to even less.

Eventually his dilemma was solved. Aboard ship, someone who saw a fast promotion fading ordered a radio message to be sent, and the lieutenant took two of his men up to the black cabin, in a rather agitated hurry.

They found the cabin stinking of whisky, and Vliesser and Rogan busy smashing the equipment to pieces.

"You were the lieutenant who found them?" I said. I knew the recent Pacific tests had been joint Anglo-American undertakings, of course.

He looked at his empty glass. "I didn't say that," he muttered. "Matter of fact, I didn't say anything. I didn't say anything at all."

He got off his stool and walked, as though he had taken patient aim, straight through the door He didn't even sway. When I got to the door myself, he was nowhere to be seen.

As I mentioned at the beginning, the names have been changed to protect innocent people. Like us.

THE WARP AND THE WOOF-WOOF

A RABBIT—even a dream-rabbit—running through long grass ought not to make crunching noises like small stones being ground together. Which meant, Jeff decided, that he was being woken up.

Regretfully giving up the chase after the white bobtail, he stretched himself from the tip of his blunt nose to the end of his long and somewhat kinky tail, and grew aware of three things in quick succession. The first was an itch behind his ear, but that could be attended to later. The second was a savoury smell in the room; even if it wasn't rabbit, it had possibilities. The third was that the crunching sounds were made by someone coming up the gravel path to the front door; was now stopping and pushing a key into the lock. Master was home!

Jeff—who had been called Jeff for the good and sufficient reason that that was the next thing to a mutt—picked himself off the floor and threw himself bodily at Tom Halliday.

"Oof!" said his master explosively. "Get *down,* you preposterous beast!"

Jeff sat back on his haunches and looked up worriedly, giving the tip of his tail a tentative wag. Tom glared at him long enough to make his misshapen ears droop, and then grinned and rubbed the top of his head.

"You be careful!" he said. "You don't have to murder me to prove you're glad I'm here!"

Jeff gave one really frantic wag to show he understood, and followed his master as he went through the hall into the kitchen, doing his best not to knock over anything on the way. It was difficult, of course, because he was the kind of dog which is always too large for any room it is in—not a sensitive, snooty, pedigreed type of dog, but an accidentally-evolved one who looked like a retriever from *that* angle and a sheepdog from *that* angle, with a touch of spaniel about the ears and a nose like a Stafford. He was, in fact, none of these; he was Jeff.

"Hullo, darling," said Susan Halliday without turning round from the stove. "That tickles, but I like it."

"Good," Tom answered, and reached past her to lift the lid on one of the pans. The smell suddenly redoubled, and Jeff gave a fairly quiet woof of joy on recognising it.

"You shut up, Jeff," said Susan, poking him in the ribs with one small toe. "How did it go today, Tom, honey?"

"Pretty hectic." Tom splashed water into the sink until it ran warm, and reached for the soap. "Ferris put me through the reaction tests again this morning, and I had another session in the G-chair this afternoon, and then Doc gave me the works. I didn't know one could feel naked inside as well as out till he started on me."

"And—what did they say?"

Tom shot a sharp glance at his wife, but reached for the towel and dried his hands before answering. "They said I was in terrific shape."

"That's good," Susan said with forced brightness, and began to stir the contents of the pan. Jeff sensed that something must be wrong, and put out one immense forepaw to touch her leg. Barely in time he remembered that on the last occasion when he did that he ruined something called "a perfectly-good-pair-stockings"; he changed his mind and merely whimpered.

For a second Tom hesitated. Then he tossed the towel over the back of a handy chair and crossed the floor to put his hands on Susan's shoulders, turning her round gently. He said, "Darling, why don't you say it straight out—that you don't want me to go?"

She pulled away from him and looked down at the stove. "Of course I don't, honey," she said huskily. "But of course I *do*—because you want to, and I know how much it means to you, and I know what a happy, wonderful sort of person you're going to be when you come back to me . . . But I can't help it if I m afraid for you, Tom!"

"There's nothing to be afraid of," Tom said comfortingly. "Robot rockets have done the round trip, landed and come back safely—there's no reason why a rocket carrying a man instead of machinery shouldn't do the same! I've been up to the moon twice, and you didn't object then."

"But the moon's different! Lots of people have been to the moon, and anyway it's all barren, no air or anything. But on Mars—well, just suppose that . . ."

"Martians, you mean?" A slow grin broke out across Tom's face. "Martian monsters? You've been watching too many teleshows, my sweet! I wondered what could have got at you!"

"But——" Susan began defensively, and got no further before she found that Tom's grin was infectious. Well, really it was rather ridiculous; she couldn't stop an answering smile, and then they broke out laughing together.

Jeff, realising that whatever had been making his owners unhappy was over with, got up from the floor and did his personal dance of joy. Somehow or other he managed to knock over a chair almost at once, and when he backed hastily away to avoid it, his tail wreaked considerable havoc among pans racked under the sink.

"Sometimes," Tom said when the last echoes of the crash had died away, "I'm very glad Jeff has no dachshund in his family tree."

"How do you mean?" Susan said, wiping her eyes.

"Think how much extra trouble it would be," Tom answered as he bent to clean the mess, "if we had to go into the next room to pick up the things he'd knocked over!"

Jr-Ktuk had never seen a teleshow, and therefore had no

prejudices about Martian monsters. He was quite content to *be* one: pseudopods, palpitating brain-case, sixteen eyes and all. At the moment twelve of his eyes were registering expressions of mingled astonishment, disbelief and dismay, and the remainder were studying Ol-Pshok as though he were a singularly unpleasant sandlouse.

"*What* did you say?" he demanded. He had heard quite well, but he had so many eyes expressing incredulity that he thought he'd better make certain.

Ol-Pshok was patently very flustered. To gain time, he embarked on a complicated obeisance which would have taken him the best part of four days if he had completed it, but Jr-Ktuk was in no mood to squat on ceremony. He cut short the bow after less than three hours with an impatient wave of a pseudopod. "Speak up!" he ordered.

"Well," Ol-Pshok resumed obediently, "as you know, a year ago we were again scheduled to reconnoitre the surface of our planet on the offchance that it had returned to habitable condition. The odds against such an occurrence are, of course, tremendous, but the caves in which we have been compelled to reside for the past ninety-six and one-third generations induce a certain claustrophobia which the excursions to the surface tend to ameliorate . . ."

Belatedly Jr-Ktuk recognised the opening of the first indoctrination lecture to the young, which a fast talker had trouble in delivering in under thirty-nine hours, and gave vent to a bellow of annoyance. Ol-Pshok disappeared automatically behind the nearest boulder, while Jr-Ktuk muttered some pointed remarks about the drawbacks of promoting a pedagogue to the post of Chief Assistant, no matter how distinguished his academic career.

With commendable restraint he tore off only three of Ol-Pshok's pseudopods before he calmed down. but all his eyes showed impatience when he said, "This is your last chance, Ol-Pshok! *Get-to-the-point!*"

Since each word of the last sentence was emphasised by a bang of his head against the rocky wall, Ol-Pshok could not help but nod agreement. "Very well, then," said Jr-Ktuk, relenting a little.

"When we were surveying the ninety-fourth quadrant," Ol-Pshok stated comparatively baldly, "we found a rocket-propelled vehicle parked on a sandflat. It was apparently under remote control, since while we watched it took off again and entered an orbit which seemed to be aimed at——" He paused impressively for effect, and Jr-Ktuk was sufficiently shaken by the information so far as to let the silence last for all of an hour and a quarter before he made an ominous move.

"—Earth!" finished Ol-Pshok just in time, waggling all available pseudopods with suppressed excitement.

"Oh, no!" said Jr-Ktuk from the bottom of his cardio-vascular system.

"Oh yes!" contradicted Ol-Pshok, greatly daring. "Definitely yes!"

"Anything else?" Nine of Jr-Ktuk's eyes showed deep concentration, and Ol-Pshok was startled. It was commonly known in the caves that Jr-Ktuk was too vain about his ratiocinatory faculties ever to allow anyone to see that a problem engaged more than a fraction of his attention. Nine-sixteenths was a new high.

But the baleful glare of the remaining seven eyes soon recalled him to his purpose.

"Er—yes," he went on hastily. "We found traces of five similar landings in the recent past. Our psychostatisticians, whose function as predictors of . . ."

Something warned him just in time that his enthusiasm for the ninth basic indoctrination lecture had better not run away with him. "Well, anyway, they tell me that it looks very much as though the Earthmen have got air-current of our plan to take over their planet and have decided to strike before us." As Jr-Ktuk had feared, he automatically added the associated platitude: "Eight-tentacled is it whose cause is just, but sixteen it which gets its blow in fust."

"Enough!" snarled Jr-Ktuk. "But that reminds me. I haven't had a report from the Invasion Department for two and a half generations now. Who's in charge of the department at the moment?"

"I am," said Ol-Pshok with more than a trace of pride.

That was too much.

When Jr-Ktuk had finished burying the remains, he stuck a pseudopod down the communications aperture in the wall of the throne-cave, and sent for Wy-Thob, formerly deputy chief and now full chief of the Invasion Department. He liked Wy-Thob considerably more than he had liked Ol-Pshok, and therefore waited with only a little bad grace while Wy-Thob performed the six-day-long wave of farewell over his predecessor's grave.

"Now," said Jr-Ktuk when the formality was over, "how about a progress report? And remember: Ol-Pshok's worst fault was taking his time."

"Things aren't so dusty," the new department chief said.

"As a matter of fact, Tlo-Krog tipped me the closing of half his eyes about this missile from Earth, so I ordered a reconnaissance to find out what the Earthmen were actually up to. We only finished it three months ago, but the information is already on the way to you."

"Fast work," said Jr-Ktuk approvingly. "What did you find?"

"They don't apparently plan a full-scale invasion yet. They've gone to a great deal of trouble to prepare a being called Tomalliday for the job. Odd names the Earthmen give themselves," he added in passing, and Jr-Ktuk frowned. Only in the job for a couple of weeks, and here he was developing the habit of wandering off down sidetracks instead of sticking to the point at issue.

"However," pursued Wy-Thob, oblivious of the risk he was running, "we've established this being's location, and we know he's the only one they intend to send here."

"By rocket, I suppose," said Jr-Ktuk musingly.

"Of course." Wy-Thob looked reminiscent with three of his eyes. "You know, it's just as well the Earthmen haven't discovered the spacewarp, or they'd have overrun us already. It's so much easier to send something away from the sun—downhill, as you might say—but as for the other direction . . . well, as you know we've been working on the invasion problem for sixty-three generations without getting anywhere, least of all to Earth." He chuckled with all his mouths at once, which was abominably bad manners in the presence of a superior, and Jr-Ktuk tore off two of his pseudopods as punishment. Slightly chastened, Wy-Thob went on—as soon as he could.

"As I was saying, the Earthmen are very close to achieving their object."

"But they're sending only one being?" Jr-Ktuk pressed.

Wy-Thob signified assent.

"Fine!" said Jr-Ktuk energetically. "You will arrange to spacewarp him here. The loss of the being they have trained for the trip will subject them to delay and give your department an inhaling space in which to produce the results your late unlamented predecessor did not get."

Wy-Thob turned maroon with astonishment, but Jr-Ktuk pursued relentlessly, "In order to make certain nothing goes wrong, I propose to supervise the operation myself. Come on!"

Following his superior out of the throne-cave at a respectful distance, Wy-Thob was thoughtful. He had long ago come to the conclusion that since the only possible reason for invading another planet was to dispossess the original owners and since the Earthmen were only planning to send a single individual in their rocket, they must be certain that one of their kind could handle the whole job. Consequently attendance at the opening of a warp containing that Earthman would be dangerous. He said nothing, chiefly because prior to the decease of Ol-Pshok he had been six hundred and eighth in line for Jr-Ktuk's job, whereas now he was six hundred and seventh. The future looked rosy.

Jr-Ktuk was obviously going through one of his periods of self-abnegation, because they ran all the way from the throne-cave to the Invasion Department on the other side of the planet, arriving less than a month later. The business of setting up the warp was easy; they had so many machines arranged to send Martians to Earth—which was impossible—that they could have spared dozens of them to be reversed. One was all they needed for Jr-Ktuk's plan. Barely three days after their arrival Wy-Thob cleared most of his throats and began.

"We have established," he said in a didactic tone of voice which made Jr-Ktuk look at him sharply to be sure it was he and not Ol-Pshok speaking, "that the being called Tomalliday is located at this point." He used five pseudopods to indicate appropriate five-dimensional co-ordinates. "The machine is set to transfer the living being of maximum intelligence located within a certain radius of that point. The materialisation will occur on that bench of rock over there. It is protected by glass, so there's no need to worry."

Jr-Ktuk nodded his approval, and Wy-Thob jabbed the technician who squatted at the controls in the large of his back. "You may start the process now," he said.

The complicated warp machinery began to glow and hiss and spit, and Jr-Ktuk watched it. Believing that his chief's attention was fully occupied, Wy-Thob started to edge for the exit.

"*Where* do you think you're going?" said Jr-Ktuk sternly, reaching out a pseudopod so long he would surely have torn it off a subordinate. Since he was junior to no one he could extrude it with impunity.

"Oh . . . well . . ." hedged Wy-Thob, realising too late that Jr-Ktuk's reputation for multiple attention was well-founded, "I was—uh—that is, check the power supply . . ."

Jr-Ktuk subjected him to a withering glare from all his

eyes. There was a short pause of an hour or two. Finally he spoke.

"How large a radius is your machine set for, Wy-Thob?" he asked in a dreadfully silky tone. "How big, in other words, is this Earthman?"

In spite of knowing what he was in for, Wy-Thob flinched when he glanced at the materialisation bench. He calmed himself with an effort.

"L-look for yourself!" he suggested, waving a pseudopod at the alien which had just arrived. Jr-Ktuk spared one eye to do so.

The shock was so great that he involuntarily brought all his eyes to bear a moment later, and Wy-Thob, ultramarine with relief, seized his chance to break the current record for the distance between himself and the door, leaving the hapless technician and Jr-Ktuk to face the danger on their own.

There was a long silence. Then Jr-Ktuk remembered that he was supposed to set an example. White-carapaced, he said, "What—a—*monster!*"

"This has been a lovely evening, darling," said Susan Halliday, snuggling up to her husband as they walked along the path towards their bungalow. "Hurry back so we can do it again.'

Tom slid his key into the lock of the front door. "Trust me, my sweet. I'm not going chasing after any lush Martian princesses when I have you to come home to."

She smiled sleepily. "I can hardly believe it's tomorrow you're leaving. Hasn't the time flown?"

Tom's eyes went up to the tiny racing star overhead which was the launching station. In the same orbit was the ship which would carry him to Mars. He said, "But aren't you glad the psychologists said we could carry on a normal life together till the last day? Instead of my having to be treated like a lab specimen, the way it used to happen?"

"Mmm!" said Susan, and took his hand to draw him into the dark hallway. "Hullo!" she added a moment later. "Where's Jeff?"

"Dreaming about rabbits, I guess," Tom answered lightly. "Jeff! Here, boy—we're home!"

There was silence.

"That's odd," said Susan. "Did you shut the back door?"

"I think so." Tom went forward and turned on the light in the kitchen. After a moment he called back, "Yes, it s shut.

And I closed the windows before we went out. Is he on our bed?"

"Oh, not Jeff!" said Susan. But she went to look all the same.

He wasn't on the bed. He wasn't on the sofa in the lounge, and he wasn't hiding because he'd misbehaved himself, or if he had he'd done it somewhere where they couldn't find it.

"Ah well," said Tom finally, dismissing the subject. "He's too clever by half. He must have managed to get out somehow and go chasing cats. He had his collar on, and somebody will find him and get him back to us. Come on, darling—don't worry."

Rabbits, decided Jeff, even in dreams, don't make high-pitched squeaking noises. Only mice did that, and if he was going to dream about chasing mice he might as well see what turning over would do for him. Mice weren't worth the effort, even in dreams—they were too small and too agile to catch.

He opened one eye lazily, giving his tail a brief wag for luck in case what had disturbed him had been his owners coming home. Then he forgot all his manners and scrambled to his feet, legs and tail flying in all directions. This wasn't his home!

To start with, the light was wrong—dim and reddish. And the walls should have been straight up and down, not curved as if they had been scraped out underground. For a moment he was afraid that he was having a nightmare about being stuck down a rabbit-hole, but there was nothing rabbity about this place. It didn't smell right at all.

But it smelled good.

He wagged his tail, and thereby demolished a bank of fragile equipment. The noise startled him, and he half-expected to hear his master scold him for being a clumsy brute. Nothing happened.

After a while he remembered that he hadn't stretched on waking up, so he did, and the glass surrounding the ledge of rock on which he stood proved unequal to the strain. It gave with a crash, and on turning one astonished eye towards the source of the noise he saw something move. More puzzled than ever, he extended his neck and snuffed at it.

It wasn't a mouse. On one or two occasions he had got close enough to mice to see what they looked like. This object was about the same size, true, but its smell reminded him of the crumbs of cheese he was sometimes given off the dinner table at home. He loved cheese, but the Hallidays would never give him as much as he wanted. He put out his red rag of a tongue.

Yes, *very* like cheese. He licked again. The second time was more than Jr-Ktuk could stand, and he did the only thing a good Martian ruler could do. He ran.

Not so nippy as mice, either, thought Jeff with satisfaction, putting down one of his ungainly forepaws on top of Jr-Ktuk's yell. This looked promising.

When he had finished Jr-Ktuk—who tasted *exactly* like cheese, except for the hard bits, which he left—he got down from the ledge and snuffed around. He was sure he had seen two of the cheese-creatures, but the other one had gone.

The warp machinery attracted his notice. He snuffed at it, decided there was one thing wrong with it, and put that right after the manner of dogs. He suffered a small electric shock in the process, so he trod on it to teach it better.

Then he snuffed along the trail left by the one that got away, and it led him to a gap in the wall which was too small for his body by nine-tenths. But the earth around it yielded to his experimental scraping, and he gave himself up to the task of excavation with a small wuff of pure joy. Even in his wildest dreams he had never come up with anything like this To be chasing mice which weren't fast enough to get away, and which tasted like cheese when they were caught, through something similar to an endless rabbit-burrow, was to Jeff a good preview of heaven.

A long time later a rather swollen Jeff struggled out of the surface entrance of one of the caves and looked about him, panting. The technician who got away had spread the news through the tunnels that there was a monster from Earth on the rampage, and so many of the Martians had been able to take to their own personal escape routes—some into the past, some into other dimensions, and most of them into refuges which they themselves didn't understand. They were now kicking themselves (which, with their number of legs, was quite a painful process) for not finding out about this before, instead of wasting time in stuffy caves on a dying planet. Nonetheless, Jeff had persuaded quite a few of them to remain behind.

His heaven, though, was wearing thin. He had eaten so much that he had been having to make his holes larger than usual, and he was coming to realise that with their usual remarkable wisdom and ineffable perspicacity his owners had

which was baffling many investigators; a woman could be overpowered and the moon-walker directed to the nearest Western base . . .

The pilot pushed a control home and locked it with a turn to the left; there was a slight lurch and a turning sensation, and the machine swung back on its original course in the reverse direction.

"Please—open your suit," the pilot said. Her voice was low and pleasant, and her accent good Then she gave a sudden shrill, nervous laugh, and checked herself as if she were in a state of extreme tension. "My name is Olga Solykin, and I am more glad than I know how to say!"

"Uh . . ." Well, no harm in giving his name . . . "I'm Don Bywater. Thank you for—well, saving my life."

Something was askew. Suppose this situation were reversed. Could anyone imagine missing the chance to inspect the wreck of a rival spaceship, laid out and opened like a corpse at an autopsy? Yet already she had turned the machine around and by now—to judge from the view through the excellent ports—it was making thirty-five k.p.h. back towards the base. Not a thought, apparently, for the ship.

Cautious, he cracked the suit at last. The air was sweet and good after his own canned supply, which was partly re-cycled and never completely free of his own body odours.

"Come, sit down!" the pilot insisted, patting the vacant co-pilot's chair. "Are you well? Are you hungry, thirsty? Were you injured in the fall? Were you not very lucky?"

Why was she so *eager*—almost as though she had not seen another human being for months? Her eyes were bright, and her voice tended to shake on occasional words, with what Don could only presume to be excitement. He glanced round the large cabin, noting the usual semi-personal touches—the painting of Lenin, the photograph of Yuri Gagarin, the best of Matsky-Artemov standing on a little ledge next to a package of moon maps.

The stabilising equipment was fantastic! Listening hard, he could faintly discern the hum of a gyro somewhere, keeping the cabin dead level no matter what kind of ground the moon-walker was scrambling over.

Belatedly, he began to peel off his suit. He said, "No, I wasn't hurt, thank you. I was very lucky. The whole of my acceleration unit came away in one piece and I was still in it when it hit the ground."

"I'm so glad!" the pilot cried. She turned and felt along a shelf under the exiguous bank of controls; the machine was obviously completely automatic when bound for a known destination. She produced a large box of candy and some packs of cigarettes, and offered them to him as he sat down.

He was so taken aback he forgot that it was probably bad to show that he was impressed by anything. He said, "You can smoke on board?"

"Oh yes, if not more than one person does at a time. I do not smoke, so please, you smoke if you like." She urged the cigarettes towards him, checked the movement, and stripped away the cellophane wrap with frantic fingers as though panicking to be of service to him.

The tobacco drugged? The candy poisoned? All the scores of stories which had been poured into his mind since he was a child came back to him. Anyway, he did not usually smoke off Earth, and rarely even at home.

But his nerves were shot to pieces, and a smoke would certainly be welcome. If there was anything funny about the taste, he told himself, he could throw the cigarette away after the first puff.

There was nothing wrong with it at all. It was very good, aromatic Balkan tobacco, and although it burned rather quickly in the oxygen-high air of the cabin it was soothing and welcome.

"And a drink, yes?" she invited. "To celebrate the saving of your life? I brought you food, vodka, all I could find, and the candy for you, and the cigarettes—you have not been in one of our moon-walkers before, yes? Or you would not have asked about the smoking of a cigarette!" She laughed again, the sound coming hard and harsh from her full-lipped mouth.

"Has anybody from my country?" he countered bitterly. What *was* all this about, anyway—some elaborate Mata Hari trick?

"Not even by now?" She seemed disappointed. "It is being so long, I hoped that—well, it is not really so long, I guess. Well, you will like to see all of it, then. Shall I show you how it is?" She leaned towards him, over the side of her chair, her face bright and her tongue going once from left to right across her lips.

A tentative conclusion jelled in Don's mind. This woman—or girl, maybe, for she was no older than himself—must have been condemned to some isolated post for a long tour of duty. It was exactly the kind of thing that fitted with all the half-authorised rumours one was always hearing, even more here on the moon than back home, because here was where the competition was fiercest. And the stress of loneliness must have made her mentally unbalanced. How else to explain her weird behaviour? Claiming to have brought him candy and cigarettes and vodka . . . he was no psychologist, but as guesswork it certainly fitted.

He said, not without some nervousness, "Later. In a little while, if you like." Not to arouse any suspicion; that was important. To jump at the chance of inspecting the works of the moon-walker might be fatal. The trick was to be friendly as long as possible, to find out where he was exactly, to get an idea of the controls of the machine, and then to overpower her and walk it to the nearest American base . . .

"Whereabouts are we?" he inquired, as casually as possible. "I was too busy fighting the controls to take a fix as I came down."

Well, that was true enough.

She jumped at the opportunity. Flushing a little, she put a finger on a switch before her. A previously dark screen on the control panel lit up with a set of grid-lines and a pattern of radar blips.

The grid lines moved visibly, in time with the motion of the moon-walker. Don tried not to look impressed again.

"Here, you see!" the girl said. "It navigates partly by dead-reckoning, partly by sighting on the stars. All is automatic now. We are here, and here are the Ural Mountains in back of us, and this red star in the centre, that is this moon-walker, you understand?"

"And you can—uh—steer it by hand if you have to?"

"Oh yes!"

She showed him how; she showed him the inspection hatch of the fusion engine, and the neat stabiliser which kept the cabin level—it turned out to be a bowl of mercury with hundreds and hundreds of tiny electrical contacts around the sides, from which a computer drew information about the vehicle's attitude, extrapolating to find the most probable correction the mechanism would next have to cope with. Don followed her explanations with mounting excitement; it seemed there was nothing she would not willingly tell him about, apparently for the simple pleasure of talking.

In the back of his mind, he was calculating. It would be best to take over the machine after about a couple of hours on board, before they came too close to its home base, but not so soon that her suspicions would not be lulled. Then he could easily locate the nearest American base—there were rather few in this region, for it was mainly a Soviet preserve—and then he could . . .

"Ah!" she said suddenly, and cocked her head. They were looking down through the inspection hatch over the forward radar, watching the ground-scanner weave back and forth on the far side of a pane of tough glass.

Don felt a stir of alarm. "What is it?" he demanded.

"We are coming in at my base. Listen!"

"We're *what?*" Pictures of a dozen wasted chances flashed through his mind. "But—why so soon?"

"Oh, you mean why if we are so near where you crashed did I come so long after you fell down? Why, there was much argument for and against to rescue you." She gazed at him with almost ridiculously melting eyes. Suddenly she thrust out her hand and snatched his, squeezing it briefly. "I am so glad they decided it must be done!"

"They?" Don stared wildly towards the cabin ports. Yes, it must be true. The machine was marching in between two low cliffs, towards a dark, over-roofed aperture; then it was in the shadow with the suddenness of a light being switched off, and the engine's note changed down to an idling buzz. But if this woman hadn't gone crazy from isolation, then what . . . ?

He pulled his hand away. "How many people are there at your base?" he demanded.

"Oh, there are many, many! Ninety, a hundred! But I have been so alone for so long!"

There was a noise from below—first, air hissing into an oversized lock, then the hurry of footsteps. Dazed, he said, "Alone? Are you crazy?"

"With no one to talk to, yes, I have become nearly crazy!" she asserted, nodding her dark head frantically. "They do not talk, you understand! They do not give me a single word!"

So she was a lunatic. And he was trapped. Don made a dash for the front of the cabin. But just as he was forming his intention the helmet and shoulders of a spacesuit appeared on the platform under the cabin which had previously lifted him from the airlock below. He was too close to stop himself. All the newcomer—a stolid-faced man with big shoulders—had to do was to trip him.

He measured his length on the deck. His forehead hit the base of the pilot's chair, and there was long darkness.

He awoke painfully, with his head aching and his eyes blurred, in a room that might well have been at any of the moon-bases he knew. Starkly furnished with bunks and one table, plus some lockers and shelves on which were microfilms, a reader and some recording spools, it was about as homelike as a fallout shelter.

He had a little delirium for a while before he regained full consciousness, and could not tell whether he actually saw, or only imagined he was seeing, Olga's face above his own, very pale and worried. He was confused, unable to decide whether the crash had been a dream and he was really in one of the American bases, or whether he was dead.

When things finally straightened out, he found that Olga was there, on a stool beside the bunk, watching him with terrible intensity. When he opened his eyes, she seemed to break suddenly and gave a long peal of half-hysterical laughter.

"You live!" she cried. "You are well! How wonderful!"

Memory came flooding back, and he could not tell if it was wonderful to be alive, or not. He lifted hesitant hands to touch his forehead. There was a tenderness, but nothing more, to show where he had knocked himself out.

Gently Olga guided his hands away, and swabbed the patch of bruised skin with something cool and wet that diminished the pain. She had barely finished the brief task when there was a rapping sound from the far wall.

She got up and took the three steps necessary to reach a sort of window, beyond which a stout middle-aged woman with an expressionless face was making quick pantomime gestures. As he rolled his head on one side to follow Olga with his eyes, Don saw her draw out from below the window a sliding compartment like those used in drive-in banks to protect cash being paid over. From it she took a charged hypodermic.

Once more the mishmash of tales about hypnotic drugs, secret poisons and ruthless espionage techniques flooded into Don's muddled mind, but he was as weak as a kitten and could not resist as the needle was pushed expertly home.

"It is good," Olga said apologetically. "It is for your health, you understand."

Don closed his eyes.

Some hours went by between sleeping and waking. On two occasions someone came and went at the curious sealed window, and signalled for Olga to go to the drawer below it. The first time she took out some thin broth steaming in a tin bowl and spooned it into Don's mouth; the second time, she took out food for herself, and by raising his head a little Don was able to see that a faint violet glow pervaded the box, which disappeared a moment after it was opened.

Sterile? Presumably. But—what for?

It was not until the embarrassing discovery that Olga was not going to leave this cramped cabin for any purpose whatever, even the most private ones, that he began to think back over what she had said. The others would not speak to her. She was alone among nearly a hundred companions. Why? Surely she could *not* simply be insane, because then she would not have been trusted to drive out alone and fetch him from the wreck.

When she came back from the unscreened sanitary facilities in the far corner of the cabin, he said, "What goes on? Please tell me! Why will no one talk to you? Why am I shut up with you like this when there are so many other people?"

Olga clasped her hands before her in a kind of parody of delight, drew up her little stool near the bed, and sat down close to him. She said, "Oh, it's marvellous to *talk* again! Even in a foreign language it is good! You know, I have come to where I have made recordings of my own voice and played to myself so as to remember what it is like to hear, and listen."

"Why?" Don persisted.

"The others are not talking now. I am the only one who is cured."

Don closed his eyes. This was too much. One sane person in a base full of lunatics?

"Poor friend Don," Olga said, laying her hand on his. "It is all hard to understand, isn't it? Here is the beginning. Several years ago, in Soviet Experimental Biology Station of Raznoyansk, is discovered strange symbiotic virus with some affinity for the nervous system, especially the brain. They give it to some monkeys, and they get very intelligent, amazing! Then they go mad. But so intelligent it is wonderful—I saw some of them, who learned to use tools, who could even talk a few hundred simple words about food and working. It is decided by the great scientist Bielov, director of the base, that he will experiment on himself, for it seems the virus increases mind activity. Changes readings on the encephalo——" She stumbled, stressing the syllables oddly, and got it right the second time. "Encephalo-graph, yes."

Don listened passively. All this was a long way from the moon.

"So in secret he infects himself with this virus that we call a *resonating* virus. It seems to respond to nervous activity as a sounding board to a tuning fork, do you know? As an amplifier.

"Now I was apprentice—student, yes—with Bielov. One evening I am working with a friend, Dvoriov, in the laboratory where we have monkeys, and Dvoriov suddenly cries out that Bielov will kill himself! Bielov is not there—he is at his house half a kilometre away, outside the station. But we go, because he insists, like a crazy man, do you understand?"

She was getting violently demonstrative. The words poured from her, with wild gestures to emphasise them.

"And he is taking poison, laid on his bed with a note by him! From half a kilometre Dvoriov *knew*. And that was when we discovered it was true, what Bielov said in his last note. This virus can create telepathy."

Don almost sat up. Only a stab of pain from his head made him fall back. Telepathy! Jesus, with a tool like that the East would . . .

"So all of us who had in any way been infected, Dvoriov, myself, many many more as well, were brought here to the moon, to this secret base, to work upon the antidote. We think we have got it. We think so because it was tested on myself, and for many months now I have been well, and have not suffered to be able to read a thought in another mind. And that was what was given to you. This was why Dvoriov wore a spacesuit when he came into the moon-walker to us—although I am now cured, perhaps, I still carry the virus, can still infect others. But I am sealed up here in the one room because I am the control study. It must be learned if the virus will one day die out in my body, do you understand?"

Painfully, Don worked it out. Yes, it hung together. He could have been infected by Olga as an immune but a carrier, and had been given the antidote, so was now an immune carrier himself, and—he had to get out of here. If he could just walk out, that would be enough to take the secret of the miraculous virus with him . . .

Or was this all a big lie?

Olga was going on, but he was scarcely paying attention.

"Now all the others, you see, think together, and talk no more. I must talk again—oh, I have been *so* alone since I was cured! Soon, when one year and a half is finished, and if I am still well, there will be more cures, but here it is a long way from other people, and our supplies come by automatic rockets and by robot vehicles, and all of us are of high intelligence, so perhaps the others may not after all want to be cured. They work together on many problems."

Don seized on that one. Telepathy would imply perfect espionage, perfect teamwork in research, limitless things!

"When you fell down in your ship," Olga hurried on, "it was much argued whether to rescue you. It was dangerous. But it would not have been possible to endure the knowing that you were dying, do you understand? Better to save you. Better also because without company I would go mad, and though I have no longer power to receive thoughts all the others can hear me distantly as they heard you."

Once more she clasped his hand. It occurred to him that he would probably need a friend in the enemy camp. He returned the pressure. It wasn't difficult. In spite of her mannish haircut and her rather disturbing eagerness to talk, she was attractive and female. Vague plans for exploiting these facts crossed his mind. In alarm, he checked them. It had just struck him that if he could be "overheard" at the distance of the crash, he could be overheard similarly and more easily now.

What a *fantastic* situation to find himself in!

"So you will help me to keep my mind well," Olga was saying, "and this will be good for the others, and also you will be a control for the antidote, because if you do not begin to have telepathy it will prove it also immunises, as well as cures. It is turning out so well!" she finished rapturously.

"What is it like to read people's minds?" Don demanded.

"So strange it cannot be explained. It must happen to you. Blurred—confusing—sometimes frightening. Worst and most difficult is when you are awake and near a person sleeping, for dreams are not logical. Almost, they are insane. That is why now everyone here sleeps at the same time; we have our own artificial time, and all sleep from midnight to eight hundred hours. This is by hypnosis, that all go to sleep and wake up together. No other way is possible."

Click! Don tried to keep the thought unverbalised, at least, so as to reduce the chance of it being picked out of his mind. He said, "And—are they listening to me all the time?"

"No, no! Much work is done, and they concentrate hard. I—or now you as well—we are like a little noise in the corner of a room. It is there, but you can forget it. To hear the tick of a watch at night, when your wrist comes near your ear, is easy, but after you wear the watch two days, three days, it is ignored, you understand? So with the mind you are not interested in. With many minds, it is much more difficult, for it is what you would call louder. Stronger."

So he could allow himself to think that it would be possible

waving, straining a little against full gravity, but not as loudly as might have been. The Vice-President waited at the edge of the field for the buggy to fetch Don across. Don went down to the little open vehicle with his personal escort, assigned to him on the very reasonable ground that after all he had been exposed to Soviet propaganda at first hand for some time and might possibly be a Trojan horse. But when they were aboard the driver still waited.

"What's the trouble?" Don demanded.

"The girl!" the driver replied in surprise. "This girl you lked out of her wrong ideas, this girl who gave up all for e or whatever. That's who they're mainly waiting for."

But . . ."

here was no chance to argue it out. Worried public tions men appeared in a mob, conferred with Don's escort, n the captain of the ship, with the responsible ground cers. Don caught snatches of angry remonstrance.

"Flay the man who started this story! But must do it or there'll be hell to play. Say she's sick? Won't satisfy them. Have to show her. Well, keep her away from any cameras or microphones, for pity's sake . . ."

And they brought her out of the ship. The cheering rose to a noise like Niagara.

Disgusted suddenly with the whole business, Don had to make room for her in the buggy's back seat, but to his amazement she was smiling, even at him, and with some sign of real pleasure at the welcome arranged for them. The driver turned the buggy around and drove at a suitably slow pace across the concrete towards the Vice-President, the cameras, and the press.

"Tell me, Don," Olga said in a voice bright with false cheerfulness, "did you ever stop to wonder about some things?"

"What?" Don was lost in worrying about what might happen in this ghastly situation, and about his tarnished glory.

"Why Bielov killed himself, yes? And why it was necessary to take all of us to the moon and close us away from the whole world?"

Don felt a block of ice form around his heart.

"Think!" Olga invited brightly. "All on the moon at our base were clever, sensible people, with high intelligence, trained scientists. All infected—not deliberately, by accident. For them, life is difficult but not bad. More were infected than are there now, but it was clearly necessary to ensure that the stupid ones, the untrained thinkers, were excluded. We know a lot, over our side of the world, about people in the mass. You also should know. People have lynched and rioted here, do you understand?"

Don stared at her numbly.

She turned and inspected the waiting crowd with a bright, hating look in her eyes. "Yes!" she said, and gave a nod. "People in the mass react strangely. They make less than the —what is it in English?"

"The sum of their parts."

The gravelly voice was Don's own, but it took him a w to recognise that he had spoken.

"That is correct." Bitterness coloured Olga's words. think perhaps I was sane till you exploited me—for loyalt you said. Now . . . perhaps not But I think there is a number of people here, enough to form well a *mob*."

Don's mind seemed to have congealed now. To stop buggy? To stand up and scream a warning?

"Possibly there are some people here who dislike your Vice-President. Political people are easily hated." Olga smiled a little crazy smile. "Do you think it would please the crowd if I persuaded the leader to kiss me, the pretty girl who has been brought to see error of her ways? Who would not know what loyalty means? You should know, Don."

Perhaps the antidote in the carriers' bodies had made the virus more efficient at the business of infecting others. The crowd took ten minutes to become the mob Olga had predicted; within days it was the hemisphere that was infected, and in two weeks, the world.

A BETTER MOUSETRAP

"I'D LIKE you to meet Professor Aylward of Copernicus Observatory," said Angus.

Up to that point, Captain Martinu had seriously been considering leaving the party. The band was much too loud, the dancing was far too energetic for someone like himself who was used to long periods of free fall that wasted the muscles, and the promise of fascinating people to talk to with which Angus had persuaded him to come along had not been fulfilled.

Now, though, he felt a sudden stir of interest as he shook the hand of the short, bespectacled, balding scientist. He said, "You mean you're the Aylward they named the Aylward Field after?"

"Er——" Aylward looked uncomfortable. "Well, matter of fact, yes, I am."

"As a result of which," Angus said, "I owe you my life, among other things." He ran his hand through his shock of coarse black hair, which stuck up from his head, in the currently fashionable Fijian style, like a chimney-sweep's brush.

Martinu said, "And I owe you a couple of billion dollars. We picked up a buster with your field in the old *Castor*, when I was a junior engine tech."

Rather diffidently, Aylward eyed the other's immaculate uniform. "And stayed on in the space service?" he said. "Isn't that unusual?"

"Oh, unique!" Martinu agreed with a trace of pride. "I'm the only man in the service who's picked up a buster and not immediately bought himself out of a career job. I say, is there anything I can do for you?"

Aylward seemed to be in some distress, his breathing deep and stertorous, his shoulders hunching forward. He said, "You can help me to a chair, if you will. I've been on Luna for the past seventeen years or so, and full gravity makes me terribly tired."

Martinu hastily took the professor's arm; he was in top physical condition—had to be—but even so he was quickly exhausted by a couple of hours on his feet, so he could appreciate Aylward's discomfort. Angus, as always, had vanished the moment he saw a conversation starting and gone to spark another one elsewhere.

There was a vacant double seat in the nearest of the alcoves off the dance-floor. Martinu headed for it. There was a couple engaged in violent love-making on the other seat, but he ignored their looks of irritation as he sat Aylward down. He said, "Let me get you a drink."

"That's very kind of you," said Aylward. He wiped sweat from his forehead with a bandana handkerchief matching his Mexican-style cummerbund. "A long cool one, for choice."

"Will do," said Martinu, and went in search of a waiter

He was on his way back with the drinks when Angus, a look of anxiety on his long face, pushed through a cluster of other guests and caught his arm.

"Martinu, I guess I should warn you about old Aylward. I

mean, he's a nice guy and a genius and all that, but like a lot of geniuses he's a bit nutty on one point, and unfortunately you've hit it right away."

"What? Busters?"

"Yes. He has a perfectly absurd theory about what they are and where they come from, and if you get him started on it, he'll bend your ear all night."

Martinu shrugged. "If he hasn't got a right to theorise about busters, who has? Besides, the Aylward Field got me a share in one—I reckon listening to him for an hour or two is a cheap price to pay for that."

"Damn it, I had to tell him what a buster was, once!" Angus made a sweeping gesture which spilled his drink over the back of his hand. Fishing for a handkerchief to dry it, he went on, "In fact, if it hadn't been for me . . ."

Something in Martinu's expression warned him. He broke off. "I guess I told you about that. Sorry. But don't say I didn't warn you, will you?"

Martinu grinned and walked on.

The lovers had gone, presumably in search of more privacy. He set a tall frosted glass beside the professor and sat down himself. "I got you julep," he said. "Is that all right?"

"Perfect." Aylward produced a length of tubing and dropped one end into the glass to save himself the effort of holding it up while he drank. "What are you having?"

"Slivovitz," said Martinu. "Sort of homage to my Balkan ancestry. Anyway, what brings you back to Earth after such a long time, Professor?"

"Oh, someone seems to be infringing the patents on the Field," Aylward answered. "Angus told me I was needed, so I came down. He's my agent, you know—and very good he is. I don't know how I'd manage without him. I've always found the world of commerce far more complicated than any problem in astrophysics, because it's easier to improve your equipment than yourself."

"You have quite a set-up at Copernicus, don't you? They tell me it's the best-equipped observatory in the System, and you financed practically all of it yourself. May I inquire—does the Field bring you in a good income?"

Aylward gave a tired smile. "Excellent! I never expected so much return for so little effort."

He drew out the tube from his now half-empty glass and began to run it absently between his fingers. "People sometimes ask me," he went on, "why I stick at my job when I'm wealthy enough to live in luxury on Earth. I think you'll probably understand me when I say I think I made a sensible decision." He cocked an eyebrow at Martinu.

The captain suddenly found himself liking Aylward a lot. He smiled, and as he nodded agreement his hair bobbed around his face. It was too soft for the Fijian style, so he had had to settle for curls like a Queen Anne wig, and being used to a free-fall crewcut he found it a permanent irritation. Damn these silly Earthside fads!

"I wouldn't even have come to this party but for Angus's insistence," Aylward went on. "I depend completely on him, as I said, and he does have this tendency to fly off into space over the littlest things . . . We were on the *Algol* together when we located the buster which started the whole thing. Did he ever tell you the story?"

Almost, Martinu said, "He's told everybody!" But he checked himself. For one thing, Angus's version of the story had probably been coloured by the passage of time, while Aylward's might give a different slant. And for another, though the professor's tone had been conventionally light, Martinu sensed that he was actually aching to find someone to listen to him. Angus had more than likely gone around warning all his other guests about Aylward's obsession with the buster problem.

He set his glass down on his knee. "That was when Rusch was in command, wasn't it?" he said. "Yes, I'd very much like to hear about it."

The radar tech first-class at number three screen held his breath for a long moment. When he let it out, it was to speak in a voice shaky with excitement.

"Buster, sir!" he said.

The lieutenant the other side of the room whipped around and bounded over with a hard kick at the far wall. He caught the back of the tech's chair with one hand and hung floating, his eyes wide. "Where?" he demanded.

"There, sir." The tech put his finger on a large green blip near the centre of the screen. "It broke through about ten seconds ago. I saw it arrive. And the range and mass are exactly right."

"Are you sure?" said the lieutenant. But he didn't wait for an answer before shouting to the orderly at the phone desk.

"Green, get me a line to the bridge!"

"Aye aye, sir," said the orderly unemotionally.

The lieutenant turned to the screen again. He said, "What is the range?"

"About four and a half kil, sir. Right under our feet."

The lieutenant whistled. "Well, for sure it didn't sneak up on us. Read it for relative velocity, will you?"

The tech slid cross-hairs over the screen, centred on the blip, pressed the switch of the doppler integrator. They waited the necessary five seconds and a figure went up on the dial.

"Six hundred," the lieutenant said. "Hasn't settled into its natural orbit yet. I think——"

He was going to say he thought the tech was right, but the communications orderly interrupted. "Bridge, sir!"

"Chuck it over," said the lieutenant, and picked the phone out of the air as it soared across the room He continued into it, "Ahmed, screen room watch, sir. One of my techs thinks we're on a buster."

"Hah!" said Captain Rusch sceptically. "How are we doing for white whales this week?"

"It showed up without warning on number three screen at four and a half kilomiles, sir. We haven't had a chance to check its orbit yet, but its relative velocity is only six hundred."

There was a pause. At length Rusch grunted. "Right, I'll get a 'scope on it," he said. "Bearing?"

"Oh-seven-six and a half, sir."

"Thank you, Lieutenant. I'll let you know the verdict. Don't get too worked up till we're sure, will you?"

That, of course, was a pious hope, Rusch reflected as he gave the bridge phone back to his own communications orderly. He could tell from the expressions on the faces around him. Even the normally placid Commander Gabrilov, who had been close enough to hear what Ahmed said, was showing excitement.

"Okay," Rusch said. "*O*-kay. I don't have to say it again."

Gabrilov gave a shame-faced grin and pushed himself over to the 'scope controls. "Oh-seven . . . six and a half," he said under his breath as he set them. "Four and a half kil . . . Yes, there's something there all right."

"Get it on the screens," Rusch said. "Come on now!" He felt his heart pounding faster as he glanced at the big screen mounted over the pilot board at the forward end of the bridge. A click. An ill-defined, misshapen object appeared in the centre of the square frame. It could have been anything out of the asteroid belt

There was a long silence. At last Gabrilov said, "Do you think it could *really* be a buster?"

"Well, why the hell don't you take steps to find out?" Rusch snapped.

Gabrilov coloured. "Sorry, sir!" he mumbled. He barked at the communications orderly. "Tell Warrant Officer Fisher to draw power for a laser beam! Ask Lieutenant Ahmed to stand by for spectroanalysis!"

"Aye aye!" said the orderly fervently, his eyes bright.

While they were waiting, Rusch glanced at Gabrilov. He said as though there had been no interruption, "It *could* be a buster, of course. It's some while since the last one was found, but there have been forty-five of the things, and they turned up all over the System. One was found in a lunar equilateral, wasn't it? But even if this *is* a buster, you've got to remember one thing."

"What?"

"They may not all be worth picking up. Some of them may only be lumps of iron, for instance. It hasn't happened yet, but it's possible."

Gabrilov bit his lip and looked lugubrious.

The communications orderly said, "Sir! Screen room!"

Rusch seized the phone. Gabrilov came diving over to hover beside him.

"Get this, sir!" Ahmed's voice said. "Spectroanalysis shows iron—cobalt—nickel——"

Gabrilov pulled a face, looking down at the floor.

"But also!" Ahmed said triumphantly. "Also silver, gold, uranium, thorium, platinum, osmium, iridium . . ."

He went on, but Rusch had lowered the phone.

"Number forty-six," he said quietly.

Whatever the reason for all that shouting and banging and laughing, Aylward wished they would stop it and let him concentrate. He was trying to cope with more figures than his portable calculator could handle, and running side factors in his head always gave him a headache. *Two zero six five nine . . .*

The door of his cabin slammed back and Angus burst in, frantic with excitement. The chain of figures vanished into limbo and Aylward clapped his hand to his face.

"For heaven's sake, what are you playing at?" he snarled.

"Didn't you hear?" said Angus, braking himself on the far wall with his foot and bouncing back towards Aylward. "What are you doing?"

"Trying to resolve some survey data—if you'll kindly give me the chance to finish the job." Aylward spoke with heavy sarcasm; he was an old-young man of thirty-five, with glasses and an expression which was usually mild but now was thunderous. "I never heard such a racket!"

"But we've picked up a buster!" Angus exclaimed.

Aylward sighed and pushed his papers under a clip to hold them to the table before sliding his chair back in its guides. "Is that serious?" he said. "Does it take long?"

Angus hooked a leg under the tabletop and shook his head pityingly. "Are you trying to make out that you don't know what a buster is?" he demanded incredulously. "You can carry an ivory-tower pose too far, you know!"

"All right, *tell* me what it is," Aylward snapped.

Angus rolled his eyes, but shrugged and complied. "Nobody knows what they are—exactly. They're lumps of matter that apparently drop from nowhere. Radar doesn't show them till they're well within detector range, and they think this may have something to do with the fact that they're fuller of high-number radioactives than a pudding is of plums."

"Oh, yes!" Aylward said. "Of course I've heard of them! But there haven't been any for some time, have there? What are they like?"

"Turn your screen on, and you'll see one. Captain Rusch had the 'scope image piped in for everyone to look at."

Aylward did so. The screen lit with a knife-sharp picture of a roughly spherical object, scarred across by the sweep of the high-powered laser beam. It was approximately a hundred feet in diameter. Lights from the ship were playing on it now and made it gleam against the black depths of space.

"I wonder how much we'll get," Angus said in an awed tone.

"Come again?"

"These things contain fabulous riches!" Angus gave him a supercilious glance. "So your ignorance doesn't show too much, listen, and I'll give you the background.

"The first one was found by the *Aurora* about six years ago. They couldn't believe their eyes when they saw it drop out of nowhere—a hundred-foot ball of concentrated wealth. They got thousands of tons of platinum out of it, gold, silver, uranium, and so many diamonds they practically bankrupted the commercial manufacturers. All the rest—there've been forty-five to date—have been cast in the same mould. The precious metals have more or less flooded the market, but the demand for radioactives is still high, and everyone who's found a buster has become rich for life.

"After the *Aurora* case there was a gold rush to the asteroid belt—no, don't interrupt, let me finish! But you don't seem to find busters with the ordinary planetoids; they showed up all over the System. And another odd thing—this is the first to be discovered in some years, although at one time they were being found at the rate of about two a month. Of course, this is probably a statistical accident; they're virtually undetectable until you're right on top of them."

Aylward said, "All right, all right! I remember now. Rudolf Cotteril was prophesying economic chaos, wasn't he? But in the event we absorbed the impact pretty well."

"So well you don't seem to have noticed it at all," Angus commented dryly.

Aylward ignored the jab. "Just a second," he said. He was frowning, for no reason Angus could think of. "If forty-five were found, and they were coming at an average of two per month, the rush lasted two years. You don't know the dates of the first and last reported findings, do you?"

"Huh?" Angus blinked. "Well, the *Aurora* got the first on twenty-seventh April, 'eighty-six—uh—and the *Capella* got the forty-fifth some time in March of 'eighty-eight. Middle of March—I think the seventeenth. Why?"

Aylward said, "And it's 'ninety-two now!" He began frantically unstrapping himself from his chair.

"Hey! Where are you off to in such a hurry?"

Aylward looked grim. "Not being a seasoned space-traveller," he said, "I was a bit worried before making this trip about the number of ships that have been lost lately. I looked into it fairly closely to make sure I had a statistical chance of getting home."

"What's that got to do with . . . ?"

"Since you have such a good memory for dates, you can tell me when the current run of losses started. They said thirty had gone missing in the past four years—more than in the preceding two decades!"

Bewildered, Angus said, "Sure I can tell you. The *Dubhe* was lost on the Venus run some time between tenth March and first April of 'eighty-eight."

"And the next ship to go?"

"The *Lucifer*. She vanished . . ." He broke off and bit his lip.

"About two weeks later." Aylward said, kicking himself through the door. Angus hung where he was for a moment; then he gave a gasp and dived in the other's wake.

The door of the bridge slid back with a squeal of complaint. Rusch turned; when he saw who the intruder was, he frowned. It was all very well to say that young Aylward was potentially the greatest living authority on theoretical astrophysics; it was all very well for him to want to make surveys distant from the sun—but on simple principle Rusch disapproved of non-service personnel shipping on anything other than a proper passenger liner.

However, the rosy glow attendant on the discovery of a buster had mellowed him to the point at which he did not even ask brusquely who had authorised Aylward to trespass on the bridge. He merely said, "Yes, Mr. Aylward? What do you want?"

"Angus tells me you've located what they call a buster," Aylward said. His face was pale, and his eyes were very wide behind his glasses.

"Yes, we have," Rusch agreed. A thought struck him, and he called to Gabrilov on the other side of the room. "I forgot to order 'splice the mainbrace,' Mr. Gabrilov! I imagine the men are expecting it."

"Aye aye, sir!"

"Captain!" Aylward said desperately. Rusch turned a frosty eye on him; he had jumped to the obvious conclusion.

"Don't worry, Mr. Aylward. There's enough valuable material in that thing out there to keep all of us in comfort for the rest of our natural lives. And spatial law provides that non-service personnel are entitled to two-thirds of a crewman's share. All we can do right now is stake our claim, of course, and with luck tow it into orbit at our destination. But we'll start the mining as soon as . . . "

"Captain, if I were you I'd be very chary even of staking a claim, let alone mining that thing!" Aylward regretted that force of habit had made him draw his feet to the floor, because the captain was floating a foot off it, and so looked a long way down at him.

There was a frigid silence. At last Rusch said, "Would you like to explain yourself, Mr. Aylward? If you can, that is."

"Well, it seems to me . . ." Aylward hesitated: how to make this clear? Then he plunged on. "Isn't it a fact that no buster has been reported for four years, though there was a positive spate of them before that? And didn't the start of the current run of ships lost in space—thirty known vessels and who knows how many others belonging to prospectors and freebooters—didn't this coincide with the end of the stream of reported busters?"

I said yes, because it was true. After all, the pin was there to provoke discussion with people. But I hoped he wasn't going to pick an argument at the moment, because he was clearly rather drunk.

He said, "I'm in the Navy. I'm scared. Sit down and listen."

The island lay baking in the sun like a large round cake. It was iced around the edge and all across its centre with bright white sand, decorated with a criss-cross design of felled trees, and on the sand a greeting for some giant-child's birthday had been written in the haphazard hieroglyphs of vehicle tracks. Exactly at its mid-point was a black cabin made of corrugated iron; around this, in a tidy radial arrangement, lattice-work steel towers took the place of candles. The whole was set on the blue-silver platter of the Pacific Ocean and measured rather less than two miles each way

It was an elaborate confection.

Beyond it, pegged out on the almost moveless water, there were large ships, none of them closer than fifteen miles away. Beached in the soft sand, or anchored to the atoll which ran out from the eastern side of the island a few feet below the surface, there were a few little ships. These were there to remove the men now working on the island to what was politely called a safe distance when zero hour approached. Yesterday the island had boasted over a hundred inhabitants, but most had already gone.

Now there remained a mere couple of dozen people on shore, mainly servicemen along to do the donkey-work of fetching and carrying. Already the landing-craft were being loaded with unexpendable equipment: half-tracked trucks, spare scaffolding, the tents and field kitchens which had done their best to make the island seem military and efficient during the past few weeks. But it took the black cabin to make it look like anything other than a tropical paradise.

Shortly, of course, it would be a rather more than tropical hell.

A number of boats, fully loaded, moved away from the shore. Eventually one solitary boat headed in the opposite direction. It was one of the smallest vessels in sight, but even so it was ridiculously large by comparison with the single packing case which was its cargo.

Naturally, this was no ordinary packing case. Aside from rating an entire boat to itself, it was also entitled to a guard of four men and an escort in white coveralls who sat beside it wearing an anxious expression and listening through

"By God, that's right!" The exclamation came from Gabrilov. "I'm sorry, sir," he added to Rusch. "But the *Dubhe* was the first to go since they perfected atomics, and I have every reason to remember that she vanished about a fortnight after the forty-fifth buster—the *Capella's.* I was due to go aboard, but I was held back by an ear infection."

"The odds against this are tremendous," Aylward said. He saw that Gabrilov's interruption had impressed Rusch, and was in haste to seize his momentary advantage. "Which is why I think it would be terribly dangerous to come too close to the buster. Uh—what exactly is involved in what you call 'staking a claim'?"

"Just a moment!" Rusch said. "Are you envisaging that the buster might be unstable and blow up?"

"Well . . ." Aylward looked at the floor. "There's an awful lot of reactive material in it, they tell me."

"Hmph! It can't be very sensitive, then. We spectroanalysed it with a laser beam intense enough to boil some of its surface off. What do you think, Gabrilov?"

Gabrilov was silent for a few seconds. At length he said, "Well, sir—we don't lose anything by being careful. To stake our claim, we'd normally match velocities and coast in close, wouldn't we? We're still calculating whether we have enough reaction mass to take the thing in tow, but I don't think we have, so we'll have to send someone over and plant an identification beacon—but much of the surface will be hot. I see several reasons why we should stand well off and take time out to programme a remote-controlled missile to act as a marker."

Rusch pondered. "Yes, it'd be cutting things fine to try and get something that massive into orbit at the end of this trip—I was working on the assumption that all we could do would be to mark her with a long-life beacon and come back under no-load to fetch her . . . Very well, Mr. Aylward. I'll arrange to send out an unmanned lifeboat with the beacon in it—there's enough iron in the buster for electromagnets to get a grip. And to satisfy your qualms, we'll keep our distance."

"Thank you, Captain," Aylward said. He was surprised to find, now that he'd made his point, that he was shaking all over and his forehead was slippery with sweat.

They tied the lifeboat controls directly in to the pilot board on the bridge, and Gabrilov took charge. On the screen was a split-image projection: one screen showed the view from the lifeboat itself, the other the picture from the side of the ship as the lifeboat curved outwards towards the buster.

Almost a quarter of an hour crept by on leaden feet as Gabrilov delicately manœuvred the tiny lifeboat closer and closer to the buster. Abruptly a tiny buzzer on the control board beeped and kept on beeping.

"A hundred miles," Gabrilov said, not looking away from the screen in which the buster had grown progressively from a mere spot of light to a sizeable globe. "The homer has picked it up. Shall I just let it go its own way now?"

"How far above the surface will the magnets take charge?"

"From about ten miles they ought to give a soft enough landing for the beacon to survive undamaged."

"Then try and match velocities with the lifeboat about ten miles off."

Gabrilov raised an eyebrow and looked worried, but he moved the main jet control slightly, and the image of the lifeboat in the other half of the screen showed a spurt of reaction mass.

More time limped by.

At last Gabrilov gave a precisely timed touch to the braking jet controls, and sat back. "Very nice," Rusch said under his breath. "Yes, she's going down."

Aylward wondered if his heartbeats were audible to those around him ; he was almost deaf with the rush of blood in his ears, and he was breathing fast and urgently. On the screen, the buster grew to moon-size, Earth-size, and still larger ; by now the lifeboat and the buster could no longer be seen separately from the ship without high magnification. The beeping grew to an intolerable unbroken buzz and stopped short.

"Well, she's down," Gabrilov said unnecessarily. "And it looks as though . . ."

He got no further. On both halves of the screen there was suddenly an eruption of incredible, sun-like light, as though a miniature star had been born.

"Crew's getting restive, sir," Gabrilov said, putting back the phone. "That was the M.O. with the casualty statement. One man was watching through binoculars, and he's going to need new eyes when we land, and a man in the nav section was looking down a 'scope, and he'll need one new retina. The radar tech who first spotted it has gone hysterical and needed sedation, and we have at least half a dozen cases of radiation sickness incipient."

Rusch grunted. He had been more affected by their narrow

escape than he wanted to reveal. He said, "It seems to me some of us joined the service for no better reason than the chance of sharing in a buster! The thing would have blown us to glory if we'd gone much closer. Tell 'em they're lucky to be alive. Did the thing leave any débris, by the way?"

"Not a scrap," said Gabrilov gloomily. "Oh, there's probably some dust hell-bent for the stars, but nothing big enough to pick up on radar."

"It can't have been a total-conversion reaction!" The idea seemed to hit Rusch like a physical blow.

"No—or even at this distance, we wouldn't have survived to talk about it." Gabrilov drew himself down to a chair and formed his body into a posture, as though resting on the seat. After a moment, he said, "Lieutenant Ahmed was talking about space-mines. Weapons of war. At first I thought he was just suffering from the after-effects of seeing his dreams of riches go bang—but the more I reflect, the more I'm inclined to wonder."

Rather unwillingly, Rusch looked across the room at Aylward. "What do *you* think?" he demanded.

Aylward shook his head seriously. "I don't think it's war. I mean—well, we haven't suffered much material damage. It's cost us thirty or so ships, but we have three and a half thousand in regular service; the loss of experienced space personnel is probably more serious, but still it's a fleabite. And besides, why should . . . *someone* who can afford to disguise a mine with thousands of tons of metal and induce a reaction as efficient as the one we saw, waste effort on sowing a few mines randomly in space? They could so easily make a job of it by launching a few into orbits intersecting Earth's. No, I don't think we have to involve an enemy. My guess is that the busters are inherently unstable, being composed of such heavy elements, and conceivably they don't even belong in our order of space-time. Alteration of the nature of the space around them—on the arrival in the vicinity of a large and massive object, such as a spaceship—might upset their not very good equilibrium and blow them back into the continuum from which they came." He frowned deeply. "And yet this leaves so many questions unanswered. Why, for instance, were many of them safely brought into orbits around human-occupied worlds? I had it in the back of my mind that they might be contraterrene, but since some of them were—uh—hooked, this is out of the question. I think I'm going to give this matter some further investigation."

"Well, we can't do much here," Rusch said heavily. "We

have sick men on board who need planetside medical care, but even if we hadn't I'd order immediate planetfall. This news about busters is too urgent to keep to ourselves. Gabrilov!"

"Sir?"

"Get the nav section to programme us an orbit that will take us in radio range of a government station as soon as possible, and then home. Have the men strap down for a turning manœuvre. And you'd better have the M.O. issue decelerine, too. We're in a hurry!"

Martinu looked regretfully at his empty glass, and realised as he did so that the gentle voice of Professor Aylward had stopped. With an effort he brought himself back to the present, eyeing the other with curiosity. One would never have taken him for such a damned good story teller.

"So that was how it all began," he said after a pause.

Aylward was tying knots now in his length of tubing. He nodded. "Mark you," he said, "it wasn't easy to convince the authorities. I say, I'm sorry to have to ask you, but would you do me a favour?"

"Of course."

"Well—I'd like another drink, and I don't feel up to going and fetching one."

"Oh, certainly!" Martinu pulled himself to his feet. His muscles complained a little, but he adjusted after a moment or two and walked off with their glasses to find a waiter again. He was feeling a little superior by the time he got back—after all, Aylward enjoyed at least some gravity most of his life, whereas a spaceman like himself had to cope with the change from no gravity at all to one full gee every time he landed on Earth.

Handing Aylward his new drink, Martinu wondered whether it was genuine devotion to duty or some defect of personality which made the tubby man hide himself away on the far side of the moon. He suspected the latter, now he came to think about it. What a shame—to be so outstanding in one narrow field, and yet basically incompetent in the most important field of all, that of being an ordinary person.

With disconcerting insight Aylward said, "There's no need to be sorry for me, you know."

Martinu choked on a mouthful of his drink and began to make frantic denials. Aylward ignored him. Staring at the dancers inexhaustibly whirling around the floor, he went on, "I pity you as much as you pity me, and both of us ought to pity the people here. Like mice, when the cat's away."

Was he going to become maudlin, for heaven's sake? Martinu decided to change the subject as quickly as possible. He said, "You were saying something about convincing the authorities, Professor."

"Was I?" Aylward blinked; the alcohol was taking effect on him. "Ah, so I was! Yes, I remember a blockheaded idiot named Machin—a bureaucrat if ever there was one—who tried to make out that we'd concocted a plot to filch all future busters away from their rightful owners. Like most people, he needed to have his nose rubbed in the truth before he'd accept it. But for him, we could have saved the *Sirius*."

"I remember the *Sirius!*" Martinu said. "I had friends on her. She found a buster within radio range of Luna Port——"

"And because of Machin and his like," Aylward interrupted, "went right in to grab it, and was blown up with eight hundred people aboard. Too many people saw it happen with their own eyes, and went blind like the crewmen of the *Algol*, for that affair to be hushed up.

"So they fell over backwards to make amends. I was given facilities for taking proper equipment to the spot when the next buster appeared, and by the time the fifth or sixth one showed up, I'd worked out the theoretical pattern of the Field. They try and tell me it was difficult to do, but don't you believe it—the math is simple enough. What did give trouble was getting the generating equipment down to portable size. But we managed it in the end, made it a commercial proposition—and busters held no more terrors; we could stabilise them in our space-time long enough to cut them up and separate out the radioactives." His s's were getting the least bit slurred, and he was staring at his fingers as though unsure quite how many he could see.

"Angus tells me," he went on after a pause, "that it might have been a very bad thing. It was the direct cause of the vast inflation we underwent—when?—oh, thirteen or fourteen years ago, because the market for precious metals was saturated. It's the cause of prices like five bucks for a cup of coffee and two hundred for a taxi-ride. I remember I used to dream of having a million dollars. Now where would a million get you? I bet Angus is spending a million on this party!" He waved to include the whole of the gaiety around them. Distantly in the background a theremin was playing a solo in imitation of a trumpet. Martinu nodded pontifically.

"But of course it also cured us of the tendency to place arbitrary values on things," Aylward finished. "Now we prize only work invested as a backing for currency, and the uranium from the busters made cheap fission-power possible, so maybe the trade was a good one. Ah!"

A waiter in search of empty glasses entered the alcove, and Aylward signalled to him. "Get the captain another!" he instructed. "And one of the same for me."

Martinu hesitated, then shrugged. "Slivovitz," he told the waiter, who nodded and hurried away. A man and a girl, holding hands, looked in to see if the alcove was unoccupied, and on finding it wasn't moved away. The waiter returned with the fresh glasses.

"Foof!" Aylward said, having gulped at his. "That's rather good." He lowered the glass cautiously beside him, then leaned back, sleepily half-closing his eyes.

"Look at them," he said. "Three thousand million blind mice. Who'll bell the cat?"

Martinu, whose own wits were apparently slipping a little, said foggily, "I *beg* your pardon?"

"I said, 'Three thousand million blind mice. Who'll bell the cat?'" repeated Aylward with dignity. "Though there isn't a cat, that I know of. For 'Who'll bell the cat?' read 'The mouse ran up the clock'."

No, it was no good. Martinu didn't try to follow that one.

Aylward finished his drink with an appreciative belch, and said, "I suppose mice don't do so badly, really. What were we talking about?"

"Mice, apparently," Martinu said.

"*I* was talking about mice," Aylward corrected. "*We* were talking about busters. This can't last, you know."

"*What* can't last?"

"All this!" said Aylward largely. He gestured. "Not just this party—everything else too. All unconscious of their doom the little victims play. Tell me, do you think the human race is master of its fate, or do you believe, like some people, that we're property?"

Martinu was relieved to hear a fairly sensible remark for a change. He considered the question. "That's one of Fort's speculations, isn't it? I—well, I don't know."

"I'll tell you," Aylward promised. "Do you think you're of value to anyone but yourself?"

"No," said Martinu positively. "Nobody'd mourn me—except perhaps the crew of my ship, and some of them I'm not sure of."

"You're lucky. So am I. Just think of all the poor people who think they do matter. How disappointed they'll be when they find they don't!"

"When will that be?" Martinu said, feeling it was expected.

"Oh, definitely some time. Do you know what a buster is? I mean, what it's for?"

Martinu was finding this a little tedious. He wished he had taken Angus's advice. "Tell me," he requested resignedly.

"I warn you, you won't believe me. Angus doesn't, and he's a typical hard-headed individual, and none of the other people I've told has believed me either. Anyway, I'll tell you. You said you didn't know if we were property or not. Well, we aren't property. Because we aren't worth owning. We're just one hell of a nuisance . . .

"Did you ever find yourself bothered with mice?"

Sheer politeness, nothing else, drove Martinu to bring to bear what concentration he had left. "When I was a kid," he said finally, "I recall my mother had a house full of them. But they never bothered me. I rather liked them—except for the stink."

"How did your mother get rid of them?"

"Well, I guess we tried trapping them first, but that didn't work for long—the cunning so-and-sos soon learned to avoid the traps. So in the end we poisoned them."

Another couple appeared at the entrance of the alcove, with their arms round each other. They were too absorbed to notice that anyone else was present, and walked past the seat where Aylward and Martinu were towards the curtains hanging behind it. Glad of some distraction, Martinu glanced over his shoulder and saw that they had drawn one of the curtains back to reveal an open window ; they were leaning on the sill and staring at the stars. He envied them.

"All right," Aylward said. "Now if you wanted to do something like that to men, what would you use for baiting your traps?"

"I'm sorry?" Martinu came back with a start. Aylward repeated the question.

"Well," Martinu said, humouring him, "I'd use something either useful or precious."

"Exactly. And you'd lay some groundbait first, to lure the unsuspecting victims to the traps when they were put down."

Suddenly Martinu got it. He wondered why it had taken him so long. "You mean the busters, don't you?" he said disgustedly. But after a moment he saw the amusing side of it—and after all, Angus had warned him!

He chuckled. "So they're mousetraps, and we're the mice!" he said. "What an idea! But aren't you overlooking one thing in your analogy? How about the poison?"

stump—he liked the scent of the dried wood, and a little patient work on his arrival had turned the hole in the middle into a very passable substitute for his bed at home. Practically everything else within the four walls of his cell was from the same place as himself: Agassiz IV. Huge trailing clusters of bjao fruit dangled on the trellis masking the ceiling, dripping juice; frecatee leaves rustled to his left, nobmass stalks wove their ceaseless rhythms to his right. On Agassiz IV there was nowhere one could see bjao, frecatee and nobmass together on the same continent, let alone the same patch of ground. But Chuckaluck wasn't complaining. He had settled in very well here, and his hosts—keepers—whatever one called them—were kindly and considerate.

He emerged from his sleeping-hole with a pop like a cork from a bottle. He was about the size of a large dog, covered with fine, close fur of a shade between russet and gold—a very attractive colour, and one he often studied with approval in the mirror hidden behind the bjao trellis. He had three equally spaced lower limbs, affording him ambulation in any direction, and six upper limbs of great delicacy and sensitivity. The top of his body perceived colour—in a range differing notably from the human—but shapes he detected chiefly by the use of a kind of sonar. His sense of smell was very highly evolved, thanks to the large wet cavities under his upper limbs, through three of which he breathed.

He retired first behind a clump of ubel, also an import from Agassiz IV, and performed morning excretions and acts of self-maintenance. Then he extended his lower limbs to their maximum length and began to browse a breakfast off the bjao vine.

Madam Senior-Jones emerged from her own similar morning ritual—ablutions, cosmetinting and certain other operations still more private but necessary before facing the world—and covered a yawn, even though there was no one else in her luxurious apartment to be offended by a sight of her tonsils. The day stretched ahead of her, long, brilliant and empty. She yawned again as she dropped into her breakfast chair and instructed it to issue her Meal One, Day Nine of her current diet-chart.

Madam was her given name, not a title. Papa had been a stickler for the fitness of things. He had spent the greater part of a lifetime proving beyond reasonable doubt that his branch of the Jones family was the original one with which everyone else attempted to keep up; even after he adopted the hyphenated Senior in front of his name, however, other people resolutely refused to show him the deference due to a family tree of such eminence.

Fuming at the thought that his beloved daughter might have to go through life being treated like any ordinary person, he cast about for some means of insuring against this. Inspired by his own name—which was Adam, in honour of his most distant forefather—he hit on the ingenious device of giving her the name she now bore; it struck him as ideally appropriate, both because it rhymed with his own, and because it was a title so generally indicative of superiority that it had been used even when addressing queens.

On discovering, belatedly, the other main meaning of the word he died of shame and mortification. But he had survived long enough to instil in the child a sense of the fitness of things nearly as intense as his own, and she had spent her entire leisured adult existence in setting right things which were none of her concern.

The tiring campaign to have the shelf-brackets in the left aisle-store of the city library coppered instead of chromed—more suitable to the genuine antique books in that wing, some of which had cloth and even leather bindings—had been successfully concluded two weeks before. She had recovered more quickly than she expected from this immense expenditure of effort, and had already mentioned to her most intimate friends her desire to get back into the swing of events soon. With much clucking of tongues and wondering how she ever found the energy, they then changed the subject.

Clearly, subjects for action were in short supply right now.

The chair delivered the meal recommended by the diet-chart—maximum energy, minimum calories—and also, to her surprise, an envelope bearing her address. She couldn't remember when she had last received a message other than via videophone; it was such a strain on most people to compose words into grammatical sentences with a writing machine, and so much more pleasant to sit for an hour or two chatting with a coloured image before one to remind one of whom one was talking . . .

She turned the envelope over, puzzled, and it opened itself, dropping on her ample lap two enclosures. The first was brief to the point of curtness, and ran simply:

In view of the name you bear and the worthy opinions you hold on matters of public concern I think you should see this and possibly take action!

There was no signature. But on studying the second

enclosure, Madam Senior-Jones was quite prepared to forgive that. Why, even someone of her iron nerve would be shaken by the blatancy, the crudity, the savagery, the primitivism of it all!

Tears filled her eyes as she reflected how near this cause had been to dear Papa's heart, and how grossly she had dishonoured his memory by letting the matter rest for so long. Why, it must be years since she gave a thought to the fate of our dumb cousins . . . !

Resolution filled her, to such unprecedented effect that within two hours she had not only spoken to eight of her old campaigning associates—those who had proved most indefatigable in the library affairs and others similar—but also dressed in an outfit about which she did not immediately change her mind and take off again.

She left her apartment and set off for N.A.S.E.E.Z., brandishing the offending second enclosure. It was a gaudy come-on pamphlet explaining about the record-breaking Coincidence Day.

N.A.S.E.E.Z. was not a large zoo by twenty-fifth century standards—nothing like Outback Australia or Siberia-Mars. It could boast no more than two or three thousand alien exhibits, grouped in some fifty presentations. But it was the best-attended zoo on Earth for two excellent reasons: it was nearer to large centres of population than any other E.Z., and it had been able to select those exhibits which were most interesting to the casual sightseer. Outback and Siberia, the purpose of whose existence was to conduct research into the biology and metabolism of the alien creatures they housed, were hard to get to and rather dull if one did bother to make the trip. Free from this particular obligation, N.A.S.E.E.Z. had been able to organise its material far more attractively.

True, it was necessary to separate exhibits and visitors by physical barriers. Many of the aliens breathed chlorine, some cyanide, and few could tolerate more than one per cent oxygen. This disadvantage was felt keenly by people who had been accustomed since childhood of riding lion-back, wrestling crocodiles and braiding rattlesnake necklaces—the common attractions at old-fashioned Terrestrial Zoos—and who expected to be able to do corresponding things with alien beasts at N.A.S.E.E.Z. Of course, oxygen-breathing creatures could be allowed to enter the immediate presence of visitors; one such at present in residence was Chuckaluck, and very popular he had proved.

Few people, however, left N.A.S.E.E.Z. disappointed, despite this drawback. A tour of the premises was made interesting by every possible device. Alien visual spectra, for instance, to one side or the other of the human range, allowed bizarre lighting effects, often brilliant ones, which the aliens did not perceive and hence were not bothered by. Lighting for exotic shadow shapes and hypnotic textures; fluctuation in the field strength of artificial gravities, giving a sensation of being on other planets; discreet aromas in the air-circulators; microphones to relay the curious noises made by cell occupants—all resources were called into play.

Of course, what visitors saw was only the surface of N.A.S.E.E.Z. A moment's reflection, or turning the pages of the souvenir guidebook, or the recorded explanatory voice emerging at every corner of every passageway, made that clear. Myriads of invisible mechanisms monitored the well-being of the creatures here. Atmosphere, temperature, gravity, food—this was only half the story. Some beings had digestive cycles dependent on temperature; some required special angles of illumination to prevent them developing anxiety neuroses; some could only excrete in response to special stimuli, lacking which they died rapidly of auto-intoxication . ... The list of matters attended to by the tireless machines was well-nigh endless.

Directly connected with such questions was the zoo's worst problem.

Some state of minimal activity corresponding to sleep occurred in the biocycle of all the highly-organised creatures at N.A.S.E.E.Z. Visiting hours, naturally, had to be based on local—Earthside—time, but it was no help to anyone when those who came were confronted with a series of inert lumps, even if those lumps were fifty lightyears from home.

Attempts were consequently always made to adapt the aliens to a twenty-four-hour day. Some adjusted easily; others could not at any price, being too tightly fixated on their home world's night-day cycle.

During the ten hours of a day when the zoo was open for visitors, as many as half the exhibits might be slumbrously dull. Alternatively, the cycles might chime together and the whole place become a buzz of vigorous movement, colour and sound. The latter occasions always brought visitors in hordes because they were always well advertised. For convenience they had to have a name and a definition: a Coincidence Day was one when forty or more of the fifty presentations were at day activity peak for at least five hours.

oily as his fat-taut skin. "But until I saw it with my own eyes I found it incredible that half the available resources of a planet as potentially rich as Landfall should be absorbed into —h'm—what does actually absorb it. You are—check me if the situation has altered since I was first briefed—supporting four million totally non-productive individuals!"

Lammergeier felt the first beads of sweat prickle on his skin. What he'd expected from Earth he hadn't been sure. At the very back of his mind, perhaps, after his long and bitter struggle to persuade his Planetary Council that they must doff their pride and appeal to Earth, he'd nursed a fantasy of some team of miracle-workers, who would thunder out of the sky in the latest interstellar cruiser and instantly solve the Babies problem before deciding to settle here themselves.

Instead . . .

Struggling to be both polite and firm, he said, "That's hardly a fair way to put it, Mr. Murphy. The future of our colony was predicted on a certain available supply of manpower—and womanpower too, I needn't stress that. What would you have had us do? Dig mass graves and shovel the Babies in by the tens of thousands?"

"According to what I was told," Murphy said, "they're effectively mindless, and there are millions of them. They must be the direct cause of the poor maintenance I've observed in your buildings and roads, and doubtless elsewhere that I shall discover later. Moreover, the average daily calorie intake of your people is lower than that of Earth, a shocking display of mismanagement, in view of the fact that our population is now almost as high in the billions as yours is in the millions. Correct, or not?"

"Yes! But . . ." Lammergeier's forehead was now so damp he could not refrain from mopping it. He registered Murphy's disapproval of his using a handkerchief, returned to his pocket, instead of a hygienic tissue delivered at once to a disposall. And ignored it.

"Bear with me while I try and make clear how it looks to us," he requested. "From Earth, I don't contest it must seem to reflect mismanagement. But . . .

"Oh, I'll have to go back to the beginning. Landfall has been established as a Status Two colony since the middle of last century. During our immigration period, nothing but *nothing* happened to cast doubt on our assumption that it would turn out a perfectly habitable world."

"You say 'our' assumption," Murphy murmured. "You were here at the time, then?"

Galaxy! Do I look that ancient to him?

In the nick of time Lammergeier spotted the betraying twist of Murphy's mouth, and bit back his indignant denial.

A needler. But I don't have to rise to his baiting.

"I employ the word merely to emphasise the deep involvement everyone here feels with the fate of the colony." There—that was a diplomatic way of putting it! "You will hardly have overlooked that the pre-colonial stage was masterminded direct from Earth, and the government of the time was surely no less concerned for the fate of its intending emigrants than the present one which has sent you here to advise us."

Was that a wince from Murphy? Lammergeier couldn't be certain. Hoping the jab had found its mark, he hurried on.

"The—ah—epidemic, if that's what it is, which began twenty years ago came without warning. The birth of several infants who after a period of months, if not years, turned out to be subnormal could hardly have been detected while they were still unweaned, could it?"

"Interesting local dialectal variant you just used," Murphy put it. "Four million described as 'several'!"

"It wasn't four million to begin with!" Lammergeier was reddening. "This thing has been going on for twenty years!"

"And in the whole of that time, no normal infant has been born on this planet?"

"Well . . . no." Lammergeier forced out the admission in a whisper. From where Murphy was sitting, it must look like insanity to send for help only now, when the situation was out of control. Yet how could he hope to explain the real state of affairs? He, even he who had fought and won that bitter argument in the Council over so many years, felt the most violent revulsion at the idea of killing off the Babies and starting a fresh generation with adopted children from some other planet. That was the wildest idea voiced during the debate, but also the most promising. And didn't *that* sum up their predicament!

In any case, suppose it happens all over again with the descendants of the newcomers?

Murphy's eyes had wandered around the room again. Now he pointed at a faded chart hanging lopsidedly from a single pin in the wall at Lammergeier's back.

"What's that?"

Lammergeier craned around and felt a stab of surprise. That map had been there for so long, he'd ceased to register its existence—it was a background detail. In a tone of mild wonder, he said, "Why, it shows the course of the epidemic from the first township at which it was reported, to the limit of its spread."

"Which was the whole inhabited area of the planet."

"Er—yes, I'm afraid so," Lammergeier confirmed miserably.

"Fantastic," Murphy muttered. "I was reading stats of some of the advertising material distributed during Landfall's colonial phase. It makes a sorry contrast with the actual state of affairs. Well, let's not rake over dead ash right now. I shall need to see the consequences of the phenomenon with my own eyes."

There was only one place to take him, of course. Lammergeier took him there, in a wheezing car forty-odd years old held together by string, wire and the patient attention of its eighty-year-old driver. The arrival of Murphy had lent Lammergeier a fresh viewpoint, and now he thought with a shock of dismay: *Why, we're a planet of old folks!*

Nowhere on Landfall was there a functioning human being younger than the age of about forty—and the youngest were forty the way he was sixty: looking and feeling half as old again, one foot already in the grave.

He stifled the realisation and spoke aloud, pointing through the car's windshield at a building which was looming ahead.

"That's the Babies' Home for the capital and environs. The present—ah—population is about eight thousand, but as you see, we're having to add a new wing."

Murphy scowled and said nothing.

He didn't in fact speak again until they were in the lobby of the building. Lammergeier had had no chance to phone through and warn the staff of their arrival—the phone cables were out again and no one could be spared to fix them until next week. Accordingly, they walked straight into the middle of an event which was heartbreakingly typical of the whole calamitous mess.

At the reception desk, flanked by two uniformed policemen, a woman in a shabby dress stood clinging desperately to a child of about six or seven, far too heavy for her to carry yet cradled tightly in her arms. Facing her were a nurse with a lined weary face under a mop of grey hair, and a bald elderly doctor in a once-white coat.

Lammergeier whispered to Murphy, "Wait here a second, and I'll get the director to conduct you around personally."

"No!" Murphy raised a hand, eyes on the scene at the

reception desk. "What's going on?"

"Well, I assume she's what we call a 'hider'," Lammergeier explained. "Despite the fact that we don't get normal children any longer, the maternal instinct seems to be insuppressible. I suppose the two things must go together: our reluctance to face hard facts and stop trying to keep these useless Babies alive, and the refusal of so many women to part with their children. Of course, it would be ridiculous to allow them to stay with their parents. The planet's economy is rocky enough already. If members of our labour force were compelled to take time every day—and night!—to attend to their children, things would be impossible. We tie up plenty of workers by adopting the centralised system, but at least the loss to the economy is concentrated in certain districts and confined to certain professions."

"It's compulsory to bring children in to these establishments, then?"

"Oh yes—it has been for almost fifteen years. But like I said, you still get these 'hiders'."

Murphy nodded. "The children—the Babies—are literally helpless, are they? Even when they attain the advanced age at which the oldest must be by now: twenty?"

"Completely helpless," Lammergeier said. "They're exactly like babies, which is what we call them. They have to be fed, changed, lifted up and down from bed to floor so they can play a bit—they show interest in bright colours and moving toys, but that's the absolute limit of their mental attainments."

Abruptly the woman at the desk burst into hysterics. The policeman gently but firmly separated her from the child, handed it over to the nurse, and marched her out, still screaming as though her throat would split. Lammergeier and Murphy stood in silence till she was gone.

Then Murphy shook his head. "Fantastic. I'm sorry, but I find all this incredible. With the advantages of a planet that's still virgin over most of its surface, to wind up in this plight!"

"You don't understand," Lammergeier sighed.

"Maybe not. After all, I come from Earth, where a non-productive individual is a luxury we barely tolerate at all. Certainly we wouldn't tolerate twenty per cent of them in the population, nor would we go to such elaborate lengths to enable their survival!"

"But there's nothing apparently wrong with them!" Lammergeier barked. "To all outward appearances they're healthy; they're organically sound! If some way could be found of bringing their intelligence up to—if not full adult status—at any rate bright idiot level, we could let them look after themselves and what's more we'd get work out of them. They represent a tremendous potential increment to our workforce! Get them out of their beds where they lie like vegetables and we'd be back on our original development schedule within half a century!"

"And that's the miracle you're expecting me to work?" Murphy demanded coldly.

"Well—not you exactly. But we hoped that with Earth's vast store of knowledge and skills we haven't had time to bring forward on Landfall . . ."

"I presume," Murphy said with biting irony, "you've been too busy to calculate the mere time it would take to process the millions of your—your Babies, even granting such a process could be devised!"

"I—uh—I imagine it would take years, at least," Lammergeier stammered.

"At least," confirmed Murphy. "I am not here to wave a magic wand and bring your idiot children out of their overgrown crèches, as you appear to imagine. I'm here simply and solely to evaluate the situation and make a recommendation as to the future viability of our colony on Landfall. Now if that's understood, shall we proceed?"

It was fortunate for Lammergeier that from that point on he could hand over the job of explaining things to Murphy. Director Chen and Matron Hobday had all the facts at their tonguetips, where Murphy liked them. He trailed behind as they recited the statistics, identified the rooms, the endless corridors, the life-support systems which took the worst of the burden off the adult staff. Everything seemed to blur into an endless sequence of babies and Babies: the mewling puling infants and the puling mewling adolescents, a kind of blasphemy against human form in their mindless oblivion.

He only returned to full awareness when they paused before a door he recognised. It was a little more stained and the paint was more chipped than the last time he'd seen it, five years ago. But it was the same door. And the same paint.

"And this room houses the first of them," Director Chen was saying. "You'll perhaps have noticed that this is the oldest wing of the building; the remainder is entirely a series of more recent extensions. When the very first of the—ah—victims were identified, they were brought here for observation, and apart from minor alterations necessitated by their growing older and larger, their quarters are the same that they've always known."

"Such darlings they are, too!" exclaimed Matron Hobday, and added uncomfortably when Murphy stared at her, "Well—in their own way, you know!"

Chen, frowning, made to open the door. Murphy stopped him with a gesture and betrayed apprehension.

"Ah—they are of normal adult size now, are they?" he asked.

"Oh yes. Within the Landfall range of height and weight."

"And they're completely unaggressive? I mean, I should have thought that an infantile mind in an adult body was likely to lead to at least occasional outbursts of bad temper, which might be rather destructive."

"No, that's one thing I can safely say we've never observed," Chen assured him. "Had the condition led to violent tantrums I'm sure we'd have been in touch with you much earlier than this."

"I see." Murphy rubbed his chin. "And something else. How many adults and near-adults are there at present?"

"Over—shall we say fifteen years of age?" Chen suggested. On Murphy's nod, he counted to himself. "Approximately . . . three-quarters of a million. There was a peak, you see, about two years after the knowledge of our problems became widespread; our fertile parents all knew their heredity was good—they'd been checked for it as a matter of routine—so they futilely attempted to beat the odds. Later, the mood changed, and now most people have given up trying. A case like the one you saw downstairs on your arrival is a rarity these days, though as recently as three years ago it would have been commonplace."

"Good; that's all I wanted to know." Murphy pointed at the door. "Shall we go in?"

Nervously, Lammergeier followed behind. Beyond the door, things were much as he had last seen them, apart from more wear and tear. The Babies, adults in everything except mentality, were being put down for their day-time rest. The floor was marked with traces of their presence, some of the traces none too savoury, but they themselves were all in their oversize cots, cooing or complaining according to temperament. Two hefty male nurses and one woman were just settling the last of them down. Lammergeier stifled a cry of admiration for their devotion; any of the Babies would have outweighed him, and it must be a terrible task lifting and lowering them several times daily.

The nurses were surprised at the entrance of their director and his companions, but they refrained from asking questions, completed their work on a nod from Chen, and went out with curious glances.

The instant the door was shut, Murphy marched over to the bed of the nearest Baby, and stared down at him, naked except for a huge diaper. He set his memocase on the high metal rail intended to prevent the Baby toppling out of bed if he rolled in his sleep.

"And these are the creatures you've slaved to keep alive and well for twenty years," he murmured, touching the controls on the case. "I have to grant that they seem physically sound."

"Oh, they are!" Chen hastened to assure him. "They've had the best diet, the best medical care—not that they need much of that; they're astonishingly healthy. If only we could find a way to spark their intelligence!"

"You say they're quite moronic?" Murphy stressed.

"Completely! Not one of them has ever progressed to the stage of uttering a recognisable word. They coo and cry, and that's the limit of their aspirations."

"I think you must be crazy," Murphy said with abrupt coldness, letting the case fall beside him to the full stretch of his arm. He turned to confront them.

Lammergeier pushed forward. "So we're crazy, are we?" he blurted, unable to restrain himself any longer. "We should have killed them off and buried them by the thousand, should we? Oh, probably it looks that simple from Earth! But these are *our* kids, and this is *our* planet, that we've sweated and slaved over all our lives! How the hell do you think we could bring ourselves to face the need to exterminate them because they aren't as useful as animals, then pack our gear and quit Landfall forever for fear it might happen again? We couldn't! And it's no damned good trying to make out we ought to have done!"

"No, I wouldn't say that," Murphy agreed. "Man is hardly a perfectly rational animal, is he?"

Lammergeier shook his head dumbly.

"But I didn't mean that," Murphy pursued. "What I meant was that you're crazy to think these Babies are mindless."

Chen reacted first to that. He took half a pace forward. "But I assure you, Mr. Murphy, on the basis of years of experience, that that's the case! I've run every test I ever heard of—I traced every wild speculation I could locate about nonverbal intelligence, in the hope they might represent a mutation with some other faculty equally serviceable and equally human. I drew a blank!"

"Then that's where you made your worst mistake," Murphy shrugged. "I don't see that there's much wrong with these young men around us."

"Of course you can't *see* what's wrong!" Lammergeier raged. "That's the whole point!"

"Then how about this?" Murphy snapped. He rounded on the nearest Babies and clapped his hands together. "Hey, you! Get up! You've spent long enough lounging around having all your wants attended to! There's work to be done —*move!*"

The Babies turned their heads. There was a sound of sighing. Then, one by one, they stretched, yawned, and vaulted over the sides of their cots, to land bouncing on the floor: nineteen specimens of healthy muscular adulthood absurdly garbed in off-white loincloths and safety-pins.

Lammergeier, Chen and Matron Hobday were rooted to the spot, eyes goggling. Lammergeier found his tongue first.

"But . . . ! Did you know about this already?"

Murphy gave a faint smile. "You might say that," he conceded.

"Then—is the problem widespread?"

"Getting wider all the time," Murphy sounded secretly amused.

Taking it for a patronising comment on the stupidity of colonials, Lammergeier felt a surge of anger. "Well, if the problem's already known elsewhere and you came able to solve it with no more than a curt tone of voice . . ."

"And this," Murphy put in, hefting the memocase.

"The hell with your gadgetry! What I want to know is, why Earth let us stew in our own juice when they could have had the *courtesy* to let us in on the secret!" Lammergeier wanted to stamp until the floor gave way.

"Oh, shut up," Murphy said wearily. "They don't know about it on Earth, so how could they have told you? You there!"

The tallest Baby scratched his stomach absently. "What's this work you want done, boss?" he inquired in a clear tenor voice.

"What the hell do you think?" Murphy snarled. "There are three-quarters of a million of you grown to full size now. You could have done the job years ago. Head Office shouldn't have had to send me to kick you off your beds! Go on, start making up for the lost time!"

The Baby shrugged, put out both hands, and proceeded to tear Lammergeier limb from limb.

"And clear up behind you!" Murphy added, as he bent to the memocase—which of course was not one.

Head Office from Operative "Murphy"/(date untransliterable)/planet "Landfall"/(co-ordinates untranscribable):

When my grave-digging details get through, the situation here will be back on schedule. The ostensible failure of the project seems to have been due to nothing more than an excess in the mother-love component of the planetwide broadcast from the mind-blanketer. This appears to have been set too high for fear the natives would fight back against the Babies when the latter showed their hand. The precaution was needless, and what's more, it backfired; instead of resenting the burden the Babies placed on them, practically everyone on the planet lavished such care and adoration on the little monsters the psychological trigger intended to respond to parental hatred was never tripped. Consequently they stayed the way they were a full five years after they could have taken over.

In any case, the drain on the planet's resources and the exhaustion of all the intelligent adults of the native species would have rendered more than token resistance impossible. We can certainly go ahead with confidence.

Speaking of which—how are things on "Earth"? I've heard so much about it, I'd like to see it some time!

TREASON IS A TWO-EDGED SWORD

I FLOATED somewhere to the galactic north of Cos and felt miserable. No-weight had always made me queasy. But I was plucked if I was going to show it, especially in front of Gow. I tried to concentrate on watching the strategists at work and to draw some consolation from the fact that all the other Luans present were in much the same state as I was.

It was curious, I reflected, that the only race in the Confederacy to be descended from avian progenitors was also the only one that had never properly adapted to free fall. Of course, Nwala and the rest of the Prebs had lived half their lives in analogous conditions under water, but the Tubaraleens were used to four times as much gravity as we Luans, while the Humans came of simian stock and the psychologists said that the greatest fear of any creature which lived vertically by virtue of anything other than wings ought to be that of falling. Yet Gow—like the rest of his strange species—was diving around the room like a fish.

Still, the Humans had been longest in space, after all. Maybe custom had eliminated their primal conditioning.

I looked enviously at Gow. He tugged on the long soft yellow strands which covered his head in place of a comb and wattles. He was beating out a knotty point of strategy with old jen Popra, the head of our Luan delegation, and it looked as if jen Popra was being out-argued.

I would never have expected anything else, of course.

Gow looked at me between his legs. "Hey, jen Durgil!" he called. "Let me have that squadron of Prebs, will you?"

I was immediately flattered that he should know my name, since after all he was the head of a delegation, and from the senior race at that, while I was a junior nobody. With a glow of pleasure I answered, "Coming!" and unkeyed the stases which kept the squadron in question from drifting.

My wings seemed to be all talons, and to crown it all, when I eventually freed the squadron and flicked it over to him I misjudged my aim. It hit one of the intervening suns a glancing blow and missed Gow by the span of my wings. I cursed my clumsiness.

However, he reached out and caught it and thanked me before continuing his argument.

That was another thing I admired about the Humans. If I'd done the same to jen Popra, he would have bawled me out for a clumsy addlepate, but Humans were never too busy or in too much of a hurry to be polite and friendly.

From the set of jen Popra's comb I could tell *he* wasn't feeling either of those right now. In fact he was pretty close to losing his temper. Of course, I knew he'd put a lot of effort into his plan of attack, and from what I'd seen of it, it appeared to be a good one. I also knew that—like most of the older Luans—he objected to the Humans having more or less taken the conduct of the war out of our claws. But if there were flaws in his scheme, it was as well that Gow should point them out.

I felt myself growing hot around the wattles at jen Popra's behaviour. It was embarrassing. I reminded myself that he was one of the older generation of Luans; he had been hatched and fledged at a time when we could still think in terms of our own tight little universe—seven planets, a sun, and miscellaneous moons and asteroids.

I, on the other hand, was less than half his age. I'd grown up to look at things on a Galactic scale, and I wasn't so bothered about the glory of Lu—largely because Humans could do so many things a good deal better than we could. I didn't understand why jen Popra was so insistent on having his plan accepted, flaws and all, when the lives of thousands—not all Luans—would depend on it when it was put into action.

Now he was getting annoyed because Gow wanted to use the squadron of Prebs I'd just passed him to plug a gap that even I could have taken advantage of had I been attacking. Human-wise, Gow didn't argue when he saw that it was useless, but made the curious forelimb-joint movement implying dismissal which had become popular among my own people—shrugging—and suggested, "Suppose we put it to the computer?"

"Pluck the computer!" said jen Popra. I took notice of that! The computer was the ultimate authority, and if he was afraid to appeal to it that meant he was afraid he was wrong.

Fortunately Nwala, the senior Preb, put my thoughts into words for me. He swung effortlessly between a lane of stars, manœuvring his massive body with his two forward tentacles, and hung up a short distance from jen Popra.

"Why not?" he boomed. "You've got to have it computed eventually. If you think my Prebs are going into action without a computed assessment, you're mistaken!"

With bad grace, jen Popra was forced to yield altitude.

"All right!" Gow called. "Stand by for computing!"

Technicians of all four races adjusted the stases which kept the stars moving precisely in their orbits and the model ships in their tactical formation. We kicked, swung or flapped up between the stars to the wide platform overlooking the map.

It was a sight which never failed to awe me, though I made out I was as blasé as the Humans who built it—this slice of a universe in miniature. At present the map depicted our own location, a region bounded on the north by the Human system of Cos, and on the south, beyond our own base at Polga, by unnamed enemy-held suns. It looked like a good bet that we could take some of those suns away from them—about six—but only the complex mind of the computer could decide whether we could do it without weakening ourselves.

Still, to take six systems would be the greatest victory of the war, and I felt a surge of the excitement jen Popra must have felt as I watched the machine being prepared to act out the battle.

"What have you got on enemy fleet movements?" Gow asked another Human standing by at the master switchboard.

"Everything we could rake up," was the reply. "I've set the circuits for the optimum counterblow, to leave a margin for accidents."

"Fine," Gow answered. "All right, get going."

And in the confines of the map two fleets swung into battle.

Beyond, on a wall screen, the computer projected its estimates regarding the number of ships destroyed or crippled. Miniature flares added to the realism of the scene—it was as like watching the real thing as the Humans had been able to make it, and naturally that was almost perfect.

The time scale, of course, was accelerated. For the first few minutes—an hour or so, battle-time—everything seemed to be going right. The flotillas were moving in according to schedule, each making for its assigned system . . .

"Look there!" said Nwala urgently in his booming bass voice, deepened by alarm until I could barely hear it. He pointed with an outflung tentacle.

The gap Gow had wanted to plug was widening by the moment, and from the uncharted darkness of enemy space a swarm of lights representing an indefinite number of their spacecraft poured up towards us. Ships changed course frantically, and the figures thrown on the wall—ships probably lost—began to mount.

The total was at fifty-nine per cent of strength when Gow signalled to the other Human and the computer was shut off.

"Well?" he said, looking at jen Popra. "You saw what the computer had to say. The enemy could make us helpless for years by breaking through like that . . ."

"But that was an optimum counterblow!" protested jen Popra.

"Does it matter? We always have to assume, don't we, that the enemy are about as well apprised of our movements as we are of theirs."

"He's right," rumbled Nwala. "We can't risk losses on that scale."

"And why not?" said jen Popra fiercely. "Before we Luans had this kind of so-called 'help' from Humans, we won the Battle of Argmit, didn't we? We lost three thousand ships—but we took the system and we've never lost it again. Sometimes I think we Luans are the only ones with guts left!"

"Argmit was a long time ago," said Gow peaceably. "And you haven't suffered losses like that since, have you?"

"No, but we haven't won any victories like that either!" crowed jen Popra. "How long is this war to go on, anyway?"

Gow smiled. "I wish I knew. But we stand a better chance of coming out in one piece at the end if we save ourselves foolhardy risks by consulting the computers."

"The computers!" said jen Popra with a wealth of scorn in his voice. *"The computers!* Built by Humans, of course, and equally conditioned against their getting their feathers singed!"

Facarastulonga, the head of the Tubaraleen delegation, who up till now had been sitting silently within his refrigerated suit, must have hit the whole bank of studs on his speech-simulator at once, for an angry bellow issued from it. The Tubaraleens had been allies of the Humans for longer than the Prebs or ourselves, and the two races understood each other so well that they rarely needed to disagree. The insult to Humans implied in jen Popra's remark hit Facarastulonga where it hurt.

Gow waited until the echoes had died away. Then he said, "You know that's exaggerating. Now suppose we see what happens if we're a little less ambitious when we——"

Turning, jen Popra called the other members of our delgation. "Flap out of it, you! I've had enough for one day!"

There was nothing I could do but obey. I knew jen Popra's temper when he was really aroused. But I thought he was being completely unreasonable.

Looking back as I followed the other Luans through the door, I saw Gow, an odd look of pity on his face, turning to Facarastulonga. He said something which I barely heard. I thought it sounded like, "Someone's going to kick the old cock down the peck-order soon."

And he was quite right. The way jen Popra and the rest of our leaders were carrying on, what with their constant quarrelling with the Humans, one of the younger members of the command was going to start picking them off.

However, jen Popra seemed to have cooled down a bit by the time we got back to our flagship—the Grand Fleet was stacked in orbit for the duration of the conference, and we hadn't far to go. He dismissed us curtly and called an assembly of the seniors.

I was glad to be back in familiar surroundings. The high

artificial gravity and lack of perches in the gigantic Human vessel had, as always, made my feet sore before we adjourned to the gravityless map room which made me giddy, so I had two reasons for being relieved. I hurried home to the coop which I shared with jen Fazoul, one of the gunnery command staff, and spent a pleasant half-hour preening the temper out of me.

Just as I was finishing, jen Fazoul came back from watch.

"There's a real flap on!" he announced, tossing his computing-belt into his locker. "I hear rumours that jen Grobish has threatened to call jen Popra out. What's it all about, do you know?"

I told him what had happened at the strategy conference. "I think jen Popra's flying for a stall," I opined positively. "And I for one wouldn't mind seeing it happen. We'd be better off if he'd addled in the egg."

"Oh, you've got to admit he has something. After all, we *haven't* won any important victories since the Humans started to run the war for us . . ."

"They did not start running the war for us! They happened to be fighting the same enemy and offered us their facilities, which we accepted."

"Put it any way you like, the yolk has gone out of us. What do we do now when a problem comes up? Not: how do we solve it? We say: the Humans will know!"

"And don't they? They've been in space who knows how long—ten times as long as we have! Compared to them, we're fledglings."

"But they've taken our independence and guts away from us —or rather, we've given them away."

"Addled squawking!" I exploded. "Where's the sense in wasting time duplicating work that's already been done, when we can save ourselves the trouble? If people like you had their way, we'd still be flapping around in rockets instead of faster-than-light ships. We've got a lot to thank the Humans for."

"We're going to have more to curse them for, in the long flight."

I thought my temper had gone to roost; it must only have been broody. It got the better of me. "Where are you in the peck-order for the ship?" I said as calmly as I could.

"Seventeen-ninety-three," jen Fazoul answered, startled.

"Good. You're within my score. I can call you out. I do."

He looked surly, but stretched his wings and perforce agreed. We left the coop and made for the gymnasium, where challenges between junior personnel had to be settled. The seniors, who had fewer and shorter combats, usually held theirs in the quarters forward.

We reported to the physical training instructor on duty, who noted our names, confirmed that I was junior to jen Fazoul in the peck-roster and could call him out, and directed us to one of the challenge cages at the far end of the gym. It was up to us now.

It was half a year since I had last been challenged. and jen Fazoul was bigger and heavier than myself, but I had been boiling up to this most of the day, and I came out cock—bleeding slightly and short a few feathers on my right wing, but the winner.

I felt a glow of satisfaction that even a jump of eight places at once in the peck-order couldn't account for. This far down among the junior personnel, peck-order wasn't a serious measure of precedence; anybody within twenty places up or down from your own was generally regarded as your peer, because strict adherence would have meant continual re-grading of skilled jobs on a basis of physical prowess, and that would have been ridiculous. Though, of course, the top twenty or thirty places were always held by the senior officers—but that was often merely a courteous fiction.

What gave me so much pleasure was that I felt obscurely as if I had gained a victory for a cause—for the younger realist faction who had got over being obsessed with "the glory of Lu" and who had the sense to realise that our race was going ahead further and faster by taking advantage of the aid the Humans had been so kind in offering.

After all, the Tubaraleens had been allied with Humans for a couple of centuries at least, and the Prebs about half that long, whereas we were comparatively new to the Confederation. And the Prebs and Tubaraleens didn't seem to have come to any harm.

Of course, jen Fazoul and I didn't try and prolong the quarrel once we were out of the gym. He was really the fitter of us two; it was against etiquette to demand a return match, but later on he could call out someone a few steps ahead of me and get his advantage back if he won.

We went to feed together, and afterwards he went to see a match between Gunnery and Engines for the figure-flying championship of the fleet, while I returned to our coop and dozed on my perch.

I kept imagining jen Fazoul opposite me, and after a while

—more to justify myself than for any other reason—began a sort of lecture to him, reviewing the historical background of our argument.

The war had begun about forty years before, when we Luans had had starflight for less than ten years. Three systems away from our home sun, we had lost a couple of ships unexpectedly. A third one, sent to find out what had happened, returned damaged and reported being attacked. The war began as easily as that.

The enemy appeared to surround us—or at least to hold stars scattered on all sides of our home. To even the balance, we fought Argmit, and wound up with a hundred per cent increase in holdings.

While we were still preening our bent feathers, though, our fleet was alarmed by the approach of a gigantic and unidentified alien ship from a direction we had not explored. Assuming at first that it belonged to the enemy, for we knew of no other race in space, we launched panicky attacks on it.

But our weapons had no effect, and the intruders did not retaliate. When in the end we decided they could not be hostile, we made our first contact with the race called Humans —warm-blooded oxygen-breathers like ourselves.

They—as they explained to us—were also engaged in fighting an interstellar war. The race we were struggling with was one of a group allied against them. They could always do with new assistance; would we consent to join them and their associates, the Prebs and Tubaraleens?

We would. We did. It came as a shock to discover that the Galaxy was actually full of alien beings, far more advanced than we were, but after the bitter-sweet victory of Argmit we were in no mood to refuse help.

The Humans had been very good to us. They had undertaken a period of education, offering us science and knowledge which we could have spent centuries acquiring for ourselves. Our ships had gone into battle under Preb and Tubaraleen commanders until we had gained an idea of interstellar strategy, and a few years ago we Luans had been accepted as full-fledged members of the Confederacy.

No one in his right mind, I should have thought, would have quarrelled with that. It was, perhaps, annoying that the things we had been dreaming of fifty years ago should already have been done better by someone else—but on the other wing we had come ahead further and faster than we had any right to expect.

Of course, the Humans had gone the whole way by

themselves. They had been alone when they went out into space ; they had had to gain their experience without advice or aid from anyone. But they never seemed to hesitate about sharing their hard-won knowledge with us. They knew what they were doing, that was certain.

Most of us younger Luans admired the Humans tremendously for their achievements. We'd got over the stage of feeling jealous of them. The older generation, like jen Popra, hadn't. That was the real trouble.

But today I'd stood up for the enlightened, modern view. My win over jen Fazoul had been a sort of triumph for the faith. I dozed off in a glow of self-satisfaction.

I was awoken by jen Fazoul scrambling off his perch and rummaging noisily in his locker.

"What's up?" I asked sleepily.

"Big news," he threw over his wing. "One of our scouts reported enemy ships moving up towards Polga, and we're going to intercept them."

I was awake immediately. Polga was our own re-fitting station. "I'd better get down to my section," I said. "Is the call out for battle-stations yet?"

My job as clerk to the strategic department entailed operating intership contact during fighting.

"Not yet," jen Fazoul said indifferently. "You needn't hurry. They've got the plan hatched out already. There'll be a full briefing soon."

"That's quick work," I said admiringly. "Computed and all? You really have to lay it on those Humans."

"Humans be plucked," he answered with a short crow. "On jen Popra, you mean. This one, jen Durgil, is *all ours*."

He swooped out of the door and left me open-beaked.

But this was insane!

I buckled on my instrument belt and hastened through the corridors, where everything had been galvanised into frantic activity, towards my section. What jen Fazoul had said was only too true.

In the communications room, the air was full of booming voices from the Prebs—our neighbours in the Grand Fleet stack-up—demanding to know what we were doing. The officer in charge of communications, jen Katzik, a personal friend of jen Popra, was listening to them with a weary expression.

As I entered and took my battle-stations perch, he called across the room to an orderly. "Shut them off!" he commanded. "They'll find out what we're doing soon enough."

The orderly—looking mutinous—obeyed. I stared at the master chart projected on the wall and saw that the entire Luan contingent was moving out by itself, adopting a simple arrowhead formation aligned towards Polga. None of the Preb or Tubaraleen or Human ships was following us.

"We'll be massacred!" I muttered to my neighbour on the next perch, looking at the enemy fleet that was shown moving towards Polga I felt pale around my wattles.

He shrugged. "We can't just perch back and let them take Polga from us," he answered. "I guess jen Popra knows what he's doing."

"I doubt it," I said.

"If you're so sure you know better, why don't you call him out? He's only number one on the ship's peck-roster."

"This is no time for joking!"

"No time to be defeatist, either. It's up to us to show those addlebrained Humans that we're capable of running our own affairs. We've been treated as nestlings for too damned long!"

Before I could utter the hot retort I wanted, the air was suddenly filled with the sound of a Human voice from the P.A. cacklers on the walls, and jen Katzik gave the orderly who was supposed to have turned them off a savage glare.

"Hello, jen Popra!" said the cackler. "This is Gow. I'm afraid I don't know where you are in your flagship, so I'm speaking at random. I had to talk to you, though, so I've energised your public address system by remote control." A hint of a chuckle. "A trick we hadn't told you about . . .

"As soon as we realised what you were trying to do, we gave your formation to the computers. We have, actually, rather better data on the composition and formation of the enemy fleet than you got from your one scout. We've known about them for two days.

"This is the computer report. If you go into battle with your present strength and disposition, you'll be beaten. You will suffer sixty-one per cent losses plus or minus three."

An angry crow interrupted him. I recognised jen Popra's voice.

"Pluck your computer, Gow! We've talked it over, and we're sick of being treated like fledglings a day out of the egg. What I told you yesterday about the Human conduct of the war still stands. We're getting nowhere with you in charge.

"I hope some Prebs and Tubaraleens heard me say that. Though probably they're so blinded by your clever talk they won't pay any attention."

side of the chaotic battle, I heard him continue: "How about engines? How are they doing?"

"They think they can get us home, sir," was the answer.

"You—jen Durgil! Tell jen Marglu that we're crippled and have had to retire. Engines, get us out of here!"

They got us out of there. Just. The stress system of the ship had been radically changed by the damage, and as we re-materialised not far from the rest of the Grand Fleet, the Top Emergency bells started ringing. We jumped for our spacesuits.

Lifecraft from the Preb, Tubaraleen and Human ships picked us out of the mess of tangled wreckage into which the ship shortly afterwards tore itself.

Fed and rested, but feeling a depression which no amount of preening could alleviate, the survivors from the communications department, including jen Katzik and myself, sat around a large coop—or rather cabin—in Gow's flagship, which had been put at our disposal. The tattered remnants of our own fleet could not find room for us yet.

I tried to make myself comfortable on the back of a chair the Humans had brought in to serve as a temporary perch, and thought sickly that I wouldn't have to live up to my boast about calling out jen Popra. He was somewhere in the mess the missile had made of the control room.

Suddenly jen Katzik spread his wings savagely and burst out, "Why didn't they help us when they saw we were in trouble?"

"Yes, that's what I'd like to know!" said an elderly cock from Engines who had been picked up in the same lifecraft as ourselves. I didn't know his name.

Anger lent me boldness. I was about the youngest and also the most junior person present, but I spoke up. "It was our own fault!" I said hotly. "We went into something that was hopeless from the beginning We couldn't expect them to risk losses on the scale we suffered."

"Hopeless?" snapped the cock from Engines. "We diverted the attack on Polga, didn't we? They sheered off when they realised we had them spotted."

"And we wouldn't have suffered such losses if our dear 'allies' had been siding with us, would we?" jen Katzik added icily.

I subsided, and he went on, "There was something addled about that battle! I was at the conference when they drew up the plan. Our scout's report was perfectly accurate—at the time. There weren't half that number of ships heading for Polga."

"That's so," put in someone. "I handled the scout's report. There were no battleships, for one thing."

"Where did all those other ships come from, then?" said the cock from Engines. "And how did the Humans get to know about them so quickly? Tell me that!"

"Exactly," said jen Katzik. "We use Human-designed scanners and detectors. They're supposed to be the same models as those used aboard this ship. How come the Humans could know about the extra ships and we didn't?"

Defensively, since everyone seemed to be looking at me, I answered, "Maybe we didn't look in the right place . . ."

"That be plucked for an answer," said jen Katzik.

"Do we want to win this war or don't we?" said the engineer. "That's what it boils down to."

"Well!" I exploded. "If after what you saw happen today you think we stand a better chance on our own, you're addled!"

"True," said jen Katzik. "We can't win the war on our own, and the Humans, who could help us win, don't seem to want to. Where does that leave us?"

"Out of the nest and getting cold," said the engineer coarsely. The rest of the group signified agreement. My blood boiled.

"You can perch here, when the Humans have done their best to stop us making fools of ourselves and on top of that have saved our lives and given us shelter, and still say that!"

I dropped from my perch and hopped towards the door—I couldn't fly in the high gravity and narrow confines of the Human ship. I tried to slam the door behind me to underline the words, but it closed automatically

I found myself in a bare corridor—Humans never went in for fuss in their ships. There were doors at intervals, numbered in Human characters, which of course I could read, and I made a note of the one I had left so that I could find my way back. Then I started up the passage to let my temper cool off.

I must be close to the skin of the ship, I noticed, for after a few paces I passed the entrance to a lifecraft lock. I wondered if they were going out to pick up any more of us addlepated lamebrains. I felt sorry for my whole species.

I hadn't gone far when there were footsteps in the passage ahead of me, and a Human rounded a corner and almost bumped into me. I hopped back, apologising. The Human gave me a second look.

"Why, jen Durgil! What are you doing here?"

It was Gow.

Pleased, as ever, that he should recognise me, I told him, "One of your lifecraft picked me out of the wreck of our flagship and brought me in with some other Luans." I gave him the number of the cabin I'd been in.

"I should have thought you'd be more comfortable with somewhere to perch," he said solicitously. "You can't be feeling so good after what you've been through. If there aren't enough perches I can get some more . . ."

"That's all right," I interrupted, and explained why I had flown out in a huff.

"But it wasn't reasonable to expect you to risk your feathers trying to get us out of a mess we were in through our own silly fault," I finished. "So I said so, and they didn't like it. They'll get over it."

"Of course they will," he answered. He suddenly gave a sharp exclamation—the action Humans call sighing. "I wish more of you Luans would see things that way," he added. "There's no place for emotional judgments and headstrong decisions in space, you know. We've had a long time to learn that."

"How long?" I inquired, daringly. Gow seemed to be in a talkative mood, and I might never get another chance like this—to talk to a Human of such eminence alone.

"How long?" he echoed. "About seven hundred of our years."

"Where did your race originally come from?" I pursued. I had heard it said that this was an impolite question to put to Humans, but I'd never understood why; the tradition was an old one.

And, far from seeming offended, Gow merely shrugged as if the matter was of small importance. "Oh, an insignificant little planet with an ordinary sort of sun, out towards the Rim. It's gone now."

"The sun went nova?" I suggested sympathetically. For a race to bear a sorrow of that order was something which well might explain Human reluctance to discuss their origin.

"Not exactly." Gow glanced at a time-meter on his arm. "I say, your feet must be getting pretty stiff standing around under our gravity. Hadn't you better rejoin your friends?"

He was being polite—as usual—but I guessed he had no more time to spare for chat, so I thanked him and turned back the way I had come.

But I didn't want to return to jen Katzik and the others—not yet. I didn't think I'd be very welcome. So I stopped when I was out of sight and settled down on the floor. I was fairly certain I wouldn't be noticed—the Humans were surprisingly few in number compared with the influence they had, and I knew from previous visits to their ships that hours might go by without so much as seeing one of them in an isolated corridor like this one.

However, only a few wing-beats later, I heard footsteps again—two sets of them, this time—and Human voices. One of them sounded like Gow's.

I didn't want him to know that I'd failed to take his hint. I looked around and saw that the airlock to the lifecraft was close by. I had no time to think about it, but dodged hastily through.

Instead of going past, however, the Humans halted just outside the entrance.

Cursing myself for an addlepate, I dived through the entry to the vessel itself and ducked out of sight behind a row of acceleration seats just as the lock opened again and Gow came through. He was talking to someone who remained outside.

"Don't be too long," said the Human I couldn't see. "I gather jen Marglu wants to speak to you when he's feeling better. He might get suspicious if you aren't here."

"Stall him," laughed Gow. "I won't be long, of course—no longer than usual. I wish we could develop tight-band communication that would save us the trouble of personal contact, though . . . So long!"

He shut the lock and crossed to the pilot's chair without looking in my direction. Watching him fasten the harness—there was only ship gravity in here, which would vanish as soon as we took off—I wondered: suspicious of what? What was it Humans needed tight-band communication for—something they didn't want their allies to know of?

The outer side of the lock slid aside in answer to a touch on a control button, and the starry black beyond was visible through the ports facing the pilot's chair. I felt sick with fright—and sicker because I kept hearing in my mind the accusations implied in jen Katzik's words a little while before.

What was this Human secret I had stumbled across?

Gow was an expert pilot. He barely bothered to refer to his instruments as he gentled the lifecraft out of the lock and swung it up around the gigantic hull of the ship—so close, that it must have been blanked out by the mass of the larger vessel from anyone watching with a scanner. Why didn't he go out openly if he had nothing to hide?

We were still a scant wingspan from the hull when he had the boat oriented as he wanted it, and something seemed to snap in my mind as I saw that our nose was aligned towards a sector I recognised—the direction from which the enemy battle-fleet had come!

I had scarcely got over the shock of realisation, when faster-than-light drive went on. It was rough; there was no room in a little boat like this for the complex, self-compensating stressed fields mounted by a larger ship.

But then, there should not really have been room for a hyperdrive anyway.

We were going a long way. I realised that as the time ticked away. We would re-materialise well beyond the detector range of the Grand Fleet. That was another point against the Humans: why the secretiveness?

I had never before tried to look through vision ports in hyperspace. I'd heard from Luans who had, though, that it was unpleasant. It was all of that. Yet Gow seemed to mind it not at all; he kept his eyes fixed on the chaotic, seemingly patternless shapes beyond the plastic and even hummed a song, very different from Luan music but with a kind of logic to it.

By the time we re-materialised, and I saw that the stars beyond the ports belonged to the area occupied by the enemy, my mind was made up. Stealthily, I worked my way around the cabin towards the emergency toolkit. Fortunately, since lifecraft belonging to any species might rescue members of another, I knew the layout.

I had to move fast. I was bound to make a noise in a moment.

But I had the axe out of the case before Gow had done more than look round sharply, and long before he could free himself from his harness. With a quick flap I had crossed the cabin and poised the axe over his head. He wore a blaster at his belt; I snatched it away. It was made for Human hands, but I could operate it all right.

He fixed his eyes on the shining blade of the axe. "How did you get aboard, jen Durgil?" he said conversationally. "And what *are* you doing that for?"

I spoke with a heavy heart. I had trusted Humans all my life.

"Because you're a traitor," I said. "Because you knew that

we Luans were going to be beaten today. Because you warned the enemy to be ready for us!"

Outside the port another lifecraft winked into being. It matched velocities with us almost casually and started to sidle towards our airlock. I backed away from Gow, watching him and not the other ship.

"Don't try to alert our friend out there," I warned him. "I want to see what manner of being you sold us out to."

He made a move towards the radio switch; I discouraged him with a gesture. "Sit still," I ordered.

I backed into the corner of the cabin, where I could keep Gow covered without being spotted when the airlock was opened. The other ship touched with ours, and sealing tubes sprang out to form a passage between the locks.

"Open the door," I said. "Go on."

Moving slowly, so as not to alarm me, Gow obeyed, and the door slid back. A voice came through.

"Hello there, Gow. Sorry I'm late. How did your Luans come out of that little bust-up? We hurt them as little as possible, of course, but if you hadn't tipped us off the Kthalgs would have been wiped out."

So it was true. The Humans had betrayed us. I felt a wave of sour despair.

Then there were steps in the connecting tube, and I tensed, waiting for whatever alien being might come through. Gow gave me a strange look—almost pitying—but I ignored him.

And the creature which came through the door . . . was a Human.

He was very quick on the swoop. He followed Gow's eyes and turned and saw me before I had a chance to recover from my first shock, and immediately snatched the blaster away from me. It was as simple as that; my grasp was nerveless.

Gow undid his harness and got up from the chair. "We had a reception committee on board, Harys," he said with a smile. "A stowaway. It was careless of me not to make sure that the craft was empty when I came aboard, because our ship is swarming with Luans that we picked out of their wrecked flagship, but I'd met this one and thought I'd sent him safely back to his companions. Only he has a—a rather individual-cast of mind."

Harys nodded, handing back the blaster to Gow. "So that's what a Luan looks like in the flesh," he said, eyeing me with interest. "What are we going to do about him?"

"I don't know," said Gow. "You see, this one—his name's

jen Durgil, by the way—he's always struck me as being one of the most intelligent of the younger generation of his species. You know they're having the same trouble as your Kthalgs at the moment—they're still suffering from leaders who dislike the idea of co-operation."

I raised my head. "You call it co-operation?" I said bitterly. "Selling out to the enemy?"

"To the enemy?" said Gow. "But Harys isn't my enemy. He's a Human."

And of course that was perfectly true. I made an effort and got a grip on myself. "What's the explanation, then?" I said finally.

"It's quite simple," Harys spoke up. "I don't know how much you've guessed, but one thing should be clear. The war you're fighting—it is, of course, a set-up. It's phoney."

"Then what's a real war like?" I demanded, remembering jen Fazoul dead today.

"The real thing is like your Battle of Argmit, only worse," said Gow. "With a death-roll counted in billions and planets by the score laid waste forever."

"How much do these people know of our history?" Harys inquired. "As much as the Tubaraleens?"

"No. Even the Prebs haven't been given the story yet." Gow eyed me speculatively. "It would be interesting to see if he can accept it, though. Listen to me, jen Durgil. You want to know how Humans come to be fighting on both sides, don't you?"

"Are they?" I was confused.

"That's what it amounts to. You were asking me earlier where my race came from. Well, originally we came from a planet which we can no longer inhabit. We destroyed it—a long time ago." He wiped his forehead.

"We developed in an isolated sector of space. We didn't meet another race early on, as you met the Kthalgs, or the Tubaraleen met the Hravaj. But we were a quarrelsome race, and too clever for ourselves. We took over several planets around local stars and colonised them, and in the end—as we had often done before—we fought a war among ourselves.

"That war *was* the real thing. The only full-scale, merciless interstellar war we have any knowledge of. And it took us two hundred years to recover from it.

"The remnants of our race were scattered over a dozen systems. When we contacted other races also working towards spaceflight, we did our best to show them the lesson we had learned. But they weren't having any. We were forced to fight again, once or twice, to prove we didn't want to, and that was ridiculous. It seems that when a race is just discovering starflight, it's too nervous to understand that a stranger isn't necessarily an enemy.

"However, two hundred years ago we found a sort of answer. That was when the Tubaraleens were fighting the Hravaj. They had bumped each other and immediately agreed to differ. So we offered help to both sides. It was gratefully accepted.

"We couldn't stop the war—but we could take it over from them, and we did. Because we are a scattered race, we could convincingly ally ourselves with both sides.

"The Tubaraleen-Hravaj war died a natural death a century or so ago, in stalemate. They've lived with us for four or five generations now; they'll be cured of their foolish pride pretty soon, and we'll send them off to do the same for someone else. There's a battle royal broken out somewhere north of Cos between two races we haven't got around to yet."

I was beginning to catch on. I was also beginning to regain some of my admiration for Humans. "How can I know this is true?" I demanded.

"Here and now you can't," Harys said bluntly. "We can only ask you to take our word, and at the moment you don't feel like doing so. I'm afraid, jen Durgil, you've put yourself in an intolerable predicament."

"But," said Gow, "he did at least have the wit to accept the possibility of what I said, instead of ridiculing it. He's thinking with his brain instead of his feathers."

"True enough," nodded Harys.

Gow chuckled. "Don't worry, jen Durgil. We wouldn't punish you for what you've done—we've made too many mistakes ourselves. Anyway, a Luan like you is too valuable to waste." He looked at Harys. "How about finishing the job?"

"If you think it'll take this early. It's up to you—you know Luans and I don't."

"It would have to be computed, naturally, but somehow I have a feeling . . ." Gow gazed at me. "Would you like to be number one on the pack-roster, jen Durgil? I can promise you that in twenty years if you agree to my suggestion."

"Which is . . . ?"

"We'll prove to you that we are speaking the truth. It'll mean a long lonely time away from your own people, and we Humans are busy and sometimes difficult to live with. But if you want to see what we are trying to do, and then go back and help us get on with it, you can."

"I don't much want to be number one in peck-order," I said seriously. And it was true; I'd never had ambitions that way. "But I can say this: I don't see how Humans could be any more difficult to live with than old cocks like jen Popra, with all their ranting about 'the glory of Lu.' I've got no time for that sort of guano."

Harys gave a surprised glance at Gow. "How long have you been working with these people? Same time as we've been on at the Kthalgs? Gow, either you're the better worker, or these people have more commonsense than most I've met. I wish you luck—but I don't think, in this case, you're going to need it."

He put out his hand, and I brushed it with my wing tip.

"I'm sorry I called you traitors," I said. "That time I was thinking with my feathers."

"Don't let it worry you," chuckled Harys, turning to leave the ship. "The traitor who chooses the winning side becomes a hero—and in this case, both sides are going to win. So long."

EYE OF THE BEHOLDER

THE peak jutted up from the scorched range like a blood-stained fang, and its colour was indescribable. Painter knew that rose and vermilion and scarlet and crimson all entered into the total effect, for he had climbed all over it to see. It had taken him many days to survey the whole area, but he did not begrudge the time expended. He knew now precisely how the effect might be duplicated.

He was placing the first layer of pigment when the ship went past.

The movement had caught his attention a fraction before the scream of riven air came down to him, and he was quick enough to catch a glimpse of it before it dropped below the horizon. His first thought—as was natural to him—was to remark how magnificently the white vapour trail, tinted to blush-pink by the fury of the exhausts, stood out against the almost unbearable steel-blue of the sky, and to fix the impression in his mind to be reproduced at leisure.

His second was to wonder where it came from. There were

no scheduled ships visiting this world, he was certain, which left as the most likely of various alternative possibilities that it was making an emergency landing.

In which case, he might be able to help.

The passing regret at having to postpone the completion of his picture was negligible; he had an almost perfectly trained visual memory, and the colours of this mountain range were unlikely to be forgotten in a hurry.

He was a good distance from his ship, of course—he was almost at the outward end of his trek—and it would take him a full rotation of the planet to get there and back. But if the stranger was still in control of his ship, he would have put it down where Painter had put his down, for the excellent reason that it was the only decently flat and solid piece of ground on the planet. And indeed, he remembered, the line of flight of the ship had been in that direction.

There was no point in picking up his equipment. It would suffer no harm where it was, and he would travel faster for being more lightly loaded. Painter—that was his name as well as his occupation—gave a final glance around to make sure he had left nothing to be blown away, and started with lengthy strides towards his goal.

As the ship dipped into atmosphere, Froude was blaming Takamura and Takamura was blaming the mechanics at their last port of call. Christy, of course, being a woman, was blaming both of them for not organising the universe properly to suit her convenience.

Tak shot a quick look at her when he could safely take his mind off the controls for a mile or two, and wondered how long this expensive and delicate female was going to stay married to Froude. A short stay on the third planet of a B-type star would certainly do nothing to ease either of their tempers.

Froude was still shouting at him, he realised, and he broke in with a weary shrug. "All right!" he exclaimed. "You hired me to fly the ship, remember, not to service it! We can't settle anything by quarrelling now, and if you don't let up I won't be able to concentrate on the controls."

He had told Froude when the man hired him that he could put a ship down with an Alpheratzan leg-show running on the exterior viewscreen, but Christy seemed suddenly to wake up to the fact that their survival depended on the skill and judgment of Tak. She dropped into a chair and spoke in a more reasonable tone than either of the men.

"Tak's right, dear," she told Froude. "Time enough to argue when we're out of this mess."

"I suppose you've turned on the emergency distress call?" said Froude, thinking of it abruptly. Tak gave him a sour nod.

"It's been on for over an hour, since we first fell out of hyperspace."

"And how long will it take them to get to us?" Christy wanted to know.

Tak shook his head. "Five days—a week—something like that. Unless they have the stressed-space characteristics of this area on record, which is doubtful. No one's interested in visiting planets as hot as this bunch here."

Air whispered outside.

"You mean we may have to spend a *week* down there?" Appalled, Christy gazed at the furnace-mouth surface of the world as it streaked past below. "Why, there's nothing but rocks and sand all over!"

"I know." Tak was studying the radar profilometer with a frown; it seemed that the average angle of the surface was about fifteen degrees from vertical—an incredible shark-tooth mess of folds and rifts.

Froude had noticed the reading too; he quit biting his nails in the corner of the cabin—*thinking the same way as I am about Christy's reactions,* Tak commented to himself—and came over to watch the wriggling line on the screen. "You can't be going to try and land in that!" he said.

"Well, we can't just sit up here," Tak snapped ill-temperedly. "There's bound to be oxygen in those rocks, and there might even be a trace in the air, but if we stick in orbit we're going to find it damned difficult to breathe in another day or so."

"Look!" said Froude suddenly. "Over there!"

Tak saw it at almost the same instant: a patch of usable flat ground four or five miles square, cut off amid high ridges of rock and lava. Whether he could put the ship down on it after being used to the twenty-mile runways of decent spaceports, he didn't know. But he would obviously have to find out.

"Quiet!" he ordered, shooting a swift look over his shoulder to see that Christy was going to keep out of the way. She was sitting with her face set in a grim mask, and Tak guessed Froude was going to hear something from her when the two were alone.

There was only one possible approach to the level spot, between sharp-edged hills four thousand feet high. It took three passes before he gained enough confidence to attempt the touch-down, almost not daring to breathe. He was on the brink of congratulating himself, though, when he saw a smooth rise in the ground ahead—a heap of sand round-backed by the wind like a stranded whale.

Gasping, he lifted the ship and cleared the obstacle by what he suspected was about the width of his palm; then there was a slithering . . .

They were down.

He shut off the power and sat back, wiping his forehead unashamedly. The half-hope that one of the others would appreciate and remark on his achievement died as Christy got to her feet and walked deliberately over to a viewport, followed by the anxious gaze of her current husband.

She studied the landscape for some time. Then she turned and went to another port opposite. Only after that did she say anything, and her voice was full of blistering contempt.

"This is a blood-stained place for a wedding trip!"

And they were at it again.

Tak wished the ship were big enough for him to get out of earshot, but it had only been designed for the six or eight-hour journeys between stars through hyperspace, and although there were stores aboard for emergencies such as this, there was precious little else, and room was in shortest supply of all.

The quarrel died slowly. Christy had shouted herself hoarse, and crossed to the water-spigot to draw a drink. Tak's hand closed over the knob before she could press it down.

"Careful," he said flatly. "What we have has got to last a week at least. I'm going to try and rig a distillation unit, but I doubt if there's much accessible water outside."

Christy looked at him for several seconds as though she could hardly believe her ears: *hired space-pilots don't talk to me like that!* He could practically hear the thought.

Then she seemed to sag a little. She turned away. "No water," she said thinly. And the words suddenly reminded that it was getting hot in the cabin.

"I'll go turn up the refrigeration," Tak said, and stepped over to the rear door guarding the power compartment. Christy made to duck back from the sweep of the radiation field, and he gave her a humourless grin.

"This close to a B-type sun we're getting about double a safe rate already. I shouldn't let a little leak from the pile worry you."

There was none of the dismay normal to a woman who had not yet borne children in Christy's face, he noted. As he passed down the shaft towards the power compartment, he thought that if he had sized her up right it was unlikely she and Froude would be in the archetypal hurry of newly-weds, and in the confined space of this cabin it was as well. It wouldn't be sexual frustration getting her down. But what the hell? Any kind of frustration would work on a woman who had been so pampered and spoiled all her life.

Tak turned the 'frig controls over to maximum. On the way back to the cabin, he paused and reached deep into his kitbag in the baggage storebox. His fingers found the hard efficient shape of a bolt-gun immediately—he believed in having the weapon handy.

But, he reflected as he hefted it in his palm, there were degrees of handiness, and if the situation called for it, he wanted this right in his pocket.

Froude was down in the head, though Tak presumed it was nerves that had driven him there more than actual physical need, on their present reduced water-intake. He had been wondering how much longer Christy could keep up her stubborn mask.

Now her composure began to crack.

"Doesn't it ever get dark on this blood-stained world?" she demanded in a passionate voice.

"About once in three days," Tak grunted. "I checked the rotation period. We landed shortly after dawn."

"So we sit and fry till the sun goes down three days from now." Christy nodded. She started to rub her eyes, which the glare was reddening, but checked herself in mid-motion, dropping her hands to clench them in her lap.

So it's not just that Froude is scared of losing her, Tak commented. *It works the other way around as well.*

Of course, it did figure—owning an interstellar ship was a fair guarantee that a man was a good catch for any woman interested in the luxury life. Accordingly, she was going to great trouble to preserve her impeccable make-up. Tak wondered if Froude had seen his wife without it.

Peering closely, he saw tell-tale flaws appearing over her skin. Unable to wash, Christy had been patching faults as best she could. There was an end to that process.

And it might not be a pleasant one.

Froude stepped back into the cabin and shot a quick glance at Tak. Not at Christy, the pilot noted. Interesting—but nasty!